CYBORG SEDUCTION

INTERSTELLAR BRIDES®: THE COLONY, BOOK 3

GRACE GOODWIN

INTERSTELLAR BRIDES® PROGRAM

YOUR mate is out there. Take the test today and discover your perfect match. Are you ready for a sexy alien mate (or two)?

VOLUNTEER NOW!
interstellarbridesprogram.com

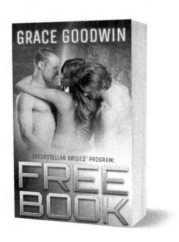

CHAPTER 1

*L*indsey Walters, *Earth Freighter Jefferson, Cargo Hold*

THE NIGHTMARE always started the same way. Sunshine warmed my face and I couldn't stop smiling. My son, Wyatt, walked beside me, his sweet little face excited as I took him to his favorite place in the world, the park near our apartment.

I wore a bright yellow and white striped sundress, one my mother and Wyatt had picked out for me on Mother's Day. Yellow daisies with green stems were embroidered into the hem. Wyatt's little blond head barely came to my waist, and his hand was warm and soft, so small and sweet in my own.

His father was long gone, a college boyfriend who'd heard the word *pregnant* and bolted like a coward. Not that it had been a big loss. The sex had been lackluster. No spark. No one had ever managed to light my fire. I hadn't heard from him, nor seen him since, and I refused to put his name on

Wyatt's birth certificate. To me, he'd just been a sperm donor who couldn't get me off.

Wyatt was mine, and I would do anything for him. Lie, cheat, steal, kill. He was my baby with pale blue eyes and dimples that made my chest ache.

Birds sang and a light breeze stirred the top of the trees. Wyatt lifted his head and smiled up at me...my heart nearly burst with love, and everything shifted.

We were in the car. Screeching tires. Explosion of glass. My baby screaming, then sobbing...then silent.

Blood. Everywhere.

The hospital, stark white walls and frowning nurses with pity in their eyes.

Wyatt's small, broken body lying unconscious in the recovery room, the doctor telling me he might lose his leg. Never walk without pain. Never run. Never play on the playground he loved so much.

My heart pounded, as it always did, but I knew this dream well. When I looked around, I expected to see my exhausted mother sleeping in the cramped chair in the corner of Wyatt's hospital room wearing wrinkled clothing and worry lines around her sharp blue eyes. Wyatt's eyes. He'd gotten them from her.

Instead of the hospital room and my mother's worried expression, a man stood behind me, his dark eyes looked as confused as I felt.

My hand burned, the odd birthmark I'd always had itching and red hot as if I'd been stung by a wasp. It hurt, but not badly. More...startling.

"Who are you?" he asked, his voice a dark rumble in my dream.

I blinked slowly and the hospital room faded. Wyatt faded until it was just me...and *him*. And God help me, he was hot. Sex-on-a-stick, I want to lick him all over, hot.

As dreams went, this was much better than Hospital 101, the dream I had almost every night. I knew that in the real world Wyatt was safe in his bed, that the car accident had been three months ago, that my mother was watching over him until I could return from this dangerous, desperate assignment. Wyatt wasn't here. This wasn't real. None of this was real.

But the man stood, motionless, like a predator watching his prey as he waited for my response.

"I'm Lindsey," I said.

He walked toward me in this nowhere place. There were no walls, no floor. It was like we stood in a thick fog, staring at one another. I held my ground as he drew closer, eager to feel his touch, eager for this fantasy that my stressed-out mind had apparently conjured, to run its course. I could use a break. And if I'd been watching the new *Superman* movie a few too many times, and my sex-starved, stressed-out body wanted to conjure up a bigger, darker, sexier version of my favorite superhero...well, I wasn't going to argue. This larger-than-life man was in *my* dream and I was going to enjoy every minute of it.

As he approached, I had to tilt my head back and I realized he was at least six-six, maybe taller, and built like a linebacker. His hair was so dark it was nearly black, his eyes a deep, seductive brown as dark as my favorite coffee but with startling golden flecks around the pupil. His skin was olive toned and flawless, a true Greek Adonis. He had just enough stubble on his face that I knew he'd leave whisker burn across my breasts if he kissed me there. My nipples tightened at the idea of those full lips sucking and tugging. He wore black boots, black pants and a black shirt that could have been from anywhere or nowhere. Non-descript, but I didn't care about the details. I didn't care where he came from, because wherever he came from, he was in *my* dream now. Mine.

Slowly, he lifted his hand to my hair, running the blond strands through his fingers as if hypnotized. I anticipated a rough touch, his size too great for anything this hesitant, but I was wrong. He was beyond gentle. He was tender, and so was his voice. "Lindsey. You can't be real."

I couldn't contain my smile. Not real? Check. None of this was real. It couldn't be. But I could feel the heat of his palm on my scalp and it almost tingled.

"What's your name?" I asked.

"Kiel. I am a Hunter."

A Hunter? Well, didn't that just fit this superhero, hot-as-hell fantasy I had going on? Yum. "Are you hunting me?"

Please say yes. Please, please, please say yes. He could hunt me, strip me, shove me up against the wall and fuck me until I screamed. I'd never had an orgasm without my battery operated best friend. No man had touched me in five years.

Not since Wyatt. Not since the sperm donor. Being a single mother made the dating thing a real pain in the ass. I was never just on a date, I was auditioning dads, and so far, none of the men I'd met were good enough for my Wyatt. And if they were? Well, so far, none of them were interested in an instant family. I was too young, only twenty-four, and guys my age were still more worried about what kind of beer they were going to drink on Friday night than taking a four-year-old to preschool and packing lunches. I had baggage, which meant I slept alone.

Except Kiel was touching me now and I wanted more. Craved it. I ached for it.

I hadn't had a dream this delicious since...well, ever.

He was staring at me, his fingers lingering in my hair, rubbing the strands between the pad of his thumb and first two fingers like he could taste me through his skin. He closed his eyes and I barely resisted the urge to reach up and touch his face, rub my palm over the stubble coating his chin. His lips were full and wide, and I wanted to touch those, too.

"I can't smell you."

That was weird. But okay. Yeah. I took a deep breath, testing the air in this weird, not real, fantasy landscape. There was nothing. Odd. "I can't smell you either."

His eyes opened, focused like lasers on my lips. "I want to kiss you."

Jeez. Was this fantasy man going to get on with it or what? As sexual dreams went, this was ridiculous. I wanted him. Now. I didn't want to talk. He didn't need to tell me what he wanted. He could just take. Oh please, take *anything* he wanted.

If he didn't get on with ravishing my body, I was going to wake up before we got to the good part. I wanted naked. Filled to bursting with an oversized cock. My body rippling in pleasure as he pumped into me harder and faster than any other man ever had.

My pussy clenched and my breath hitched. Screw this. This was my dream. I'd never been this hot for a man in real life. Never. Not once. I wasn't going to waste it.

I lifted my hands, buried them in his silky hair and pulled him down to me. "Stop talking and get naked."

God, I was a slut, but I wanted him. Bad. Dream man didn't care if I was old or young, single or married, a mother or a virgin. He wasn't going to weigh the pros and cons of fatherhood and adopting a four-year-old. If I was lucky, he was going to give me a good, hard ride and a nice memory.

Crushing my lips to his, I jumped up and wrapped my legs around his hips. His hard cock rubbed me in just the right place and I groaned, grinding against his thin black pants. I knew I was wet, so damn wet that I could smell my need drifting up between our bodies.

He was frozen under my assault and I broke the kiss, frustrated. I was going to cry. Was this just another nightmare? A new brand of torture my mind had created? Was this mommy guilt in its extreme form? Guilt for leaving my son? Guilt for taking this risk? Guilt that my son suffered and I walked away from the accident with nothing more than a few stitches?

Leaning forward, I rested my forehead against his cheek and fought back tears. What was wrong? Why wasn't he moving? This was *my* dream, damn it! And in *my* dream, this gorgeous man would ravish me, fuck me raw, make me scream. He'd want me so badly nothing would stop him, nothing would stand in his way. He'd be the ultimate caveman and he'd think I was the most beautiful, desirable woman he'd ever seen.

I whimpered, then sighed. "Come on, dream man. Please." I nibbled my way down his cheek to his jaw, felt the rasp of his whiskers against my lips. Frustration filled me because I couldn't taste him. Not really. He was warm, but he wasn't... real. I didn't care. His hands clenching and unclenching at the small of my back *felt* real. His hard length rubbing my panties felt real.

"You aren't real." He insisted, but his hands lowered to cup my ass and I moaned as heat streaked through my body.

"Does it matter?" I kissed my way to his stubborn chin, then up to his lips. I answered for him. "It doesn't matter."

I knew the second I won, felt the shift in his being. His entire body moved, flowing, pure power. His muscles rippled beneath his shirt and he crushed his lips to mine, taking what I wanted so badly to give him. I opened for his kiss and his tongue found mine, plundering my mouth with a hunger so desperate it matched my own.

Yes. Yes. *Yes!*

He tugged my dress off my body and I laughed as he

ripped away the thin scrap of my underwear. I wasn't wearing a bra, my small breasts didn't need one. With every other man, I freaked when it was naked time. I was oddly shaped, my hips and ass wide and round, my waist small, but I was an A-cup on a good day since I'd weaned my son. One more joy of motherhood no one tells you about—shrinking breasts.

But with him, I didn't care. I threw my head back and let him look as I tore at his shirt. Seconds later it vanished, along with the rest of his clothes and I thanked the dream gods for naked. Big, hard muscle, powerful physique, dark hair. My Superman. And then there was his cock....

Just as I'd wanted, he backed me up and suddenly a hard, smooth surface appeared behind my shoulders, solid and cold and unbreakable. A room formed around us and I blinked slowly, barely noticing the stark surroundings. One bed. One chair. Very utilitarian. Military. No plush pillows or thick rugs on the floor. No color, no flowers or artwork or even a design on the sheets on the bed.

Black. Gray. Brown.

I was about to comment, but Kiel's head dropped to my breast and I closed my eyes, tugging at his hair to hold him closer, demand more. His hand roamed around my ass to find my wet core and he pushed two fingers inside me without caution or warning. My back arched and I hissed at the glorious intrusion. I was tight and his fingers were big. I felt everything, the press and curl of those dextrous digits.

I nearly came all over him, my pussy clenching down on him like a fist.

"Do it," I breathed. Who was this woman I'd turned into? "Fuck me. God, just fuck me."

As if he'd been holding back still, his leash finally snapped, he slipped his fingers from me, gripped my hips to lift me higher over his cock and stopped, looking me in the eye. "Where are you?"

I blinked slowly, squirming to lower myself onto his rock hard length. Why was he stopping now? Why was he *talking*? "What?" I wiggled, but he held me pinned to the wall, his hot, muscled chest and arms holding me in place. I felt the slick heat of my arousal on my hip from his fingers.

"Where are you, Lindsey?"

My dazed mind couldn't make sense of his words. "I'm dreaming." Duh. I tossed my head back so that it bumped the wall behind me and I moaned his name. "Kiel. Please. Do it. I want you. Please."

Begging. I was begging. But I'd never felt like this before. Never. The mark on my hand burned and he lifted both of my wrists above my head as I slid down onto his huge cock. I was wet, so wet, but he was huge and I gasped. Sobbed. Shifted my hips to take more. He opened me up, filled me deep, then deeper still.

He groaned as he filled me and I lifted my head to kiss him. But he wasn't looking at me, he was looking up at my hands. Using one of his own to hold both of my wrists, he traced my birthmark with the other, the touch sending sharp bites of pleasure straight to my clit until I bucked and cried out.

He pumped into me, hard and fast, burying his face in my neck as if he wanted to smell me, scent me, soak me into his lungs. But he couldn't. Not here. There was nothing of him for me to smell. Nothing to taste. I felt treasured and cheated all at once. I could smell the wildflower scent of my favorite shampoo, smell the wet heat of my pussy as I rode him. But that was all. I couldn't smell *him*. The dream didn't let me taste him. Smell him. God, I wanted to lick him all over, rub my cheek on his chest and rub his scent all over my flesh.

I wondered what he smelled like. Pine and wood chips? Musky? Like my favorite teak and ginger scented cologne?

He entwined my fingers with his, the gesture odd and romantic and so strange I was afraid I was going to wake up. *Not now. Please, not now.*

"Lindsey," he said my name again and nipped at the base of my neck with his teeth, the added sensation pushed me over the edge and I shattered, the pulsing of my pussy pulling him deeper, squeezing him without mercy until he lost control and groaned, filled me up, his hot seed pumping into me like lava.

I could *feel* the heat of it coating my insides. And I wanted more. This dream wasn't enough.

Something jostled me and I shifted, my entire body jerking to the side.

"No!" Kiel yelled, but it was too late. Dream time was over. Something was happening to me and I needed to wake the hell up.

I tried to kiss him, to say goodbye, but he faded too quickly.

Blinking slowly, I opened my eyes and fought back tears. He was gone, and that fact hurt me a lot more than it should have. I was alone again. Not alone, as in I didn't have a boyfriend or a husband to share my life with. No, alone as in traveling through space, light years away from my hurt child. Getting farther and farther with every second that passed.

Of course, I wasn't exactly emotionally stable right now. I was scared shitless and using every ounce of courage I possessed to do what I had to do. I needed to help my son. I needed to complete my assignment and get back to Earth. I'd worked two jobs and sacrificed a lot to get my degree in journalism. And this is what it got me? Broke. Desperate to help my son. Trapped inside a shipping crate on an alien world populated with savage warriors and killers?

Any dream was better than my reality. But Kiel, the Hunter, had left my heart aching, my pussy needy. He'd made me feel something besides fear, besides hopelessness. He'd made me feel protected, cherished. Loved. He was powerful, strong enough to lean on, to accept my need and not resent me for it. But Kiel didn't exist. He was just a dream man and that hurt so much. Why was my mind so cruel?

I stared at the display screen on my standard issue Coalition Fleet battle armor. The conspirators on Earth had given me everything they said I would need. Even the bizarre technology that took bodily waste from me so that I would never have to visit the ladies' room as long as I stayed within range of their transport technology stations. That had been one of the worst 'exams' of my life. Like the gynecologist but with space dildos putting alien gadgets inside my body. A cold, creepy shudder rushed through me as I remembered the cold, clinical look of the doctor as she'd shoved that stuff inside me as preparation for my trip.

And *that* was enough of thinking about *that*.

With a shuddering breath, I closed my eyes and tried to think about Kiel instead, tried to hold onto the pleasure still coursing through my body. My pussy was swollen and hot, the pulsing of my orgasm sending aftershocks through my system. My hand burned and I rubbed at it through the gloves I wore, wondering if the mark on my palm would truly be red, of if this was some strange, lingering delusion my mind was conjuring to torture me.

My dream man was gone. The nightmare about my son's broken body was gone. And reality? Reality was staring at the inside walls of a Coalition Fleet shipping crate. No, it wasn't pitch black. No, it wasn't suffocating. I'd become used to the scent of dirt and trees from my corner where I had a comfortable chair, anchored in place. I had food and water, light.

It wasn't ideal, but they'd given me a pill to help me sleep. I was calm—too calm—and I had a feeling that special pill worked a little too well. I'd always been sensitive to medications. They probably didn't want me to freak out halfway through the journey, and I had to admit, neither did I.

If I thought about where I was going—what I had to do— for long enough, losing my freaking mind would be easy to do. I remained calm, slept, entertained myself with a tablet with movies. The perfect two-day "veg-fest" as long as I didn't think about the fact that I was hurtling through deep space in a freighter at light speed.

Forty-eight hours I'd been locked inside this cube. Yes, I had a full suit of Coalition camouflage space armor and helmet. The squinty eyed-doctor in the Miami Processing center had promised me I could survive for two weeks on the air and energy processing units built into the suit. Much longer than the two or three day journey should require.

But I wasn't sure I trusted that bitch. My head still hurt where she'd jabbed a needle into my skull to implant what they called a Neural Processing Unit, a gadget that was supposed to make it possible for me to understand every alien language I might encounter where I was going: The prison planet known only as The Colony.

The Colony was some kind of dirty little secret that no one was supposed to know about. Some of Earth's troops were reported to be there, tossed away like garbage by our own government. A few months ago, Senator Brooks from Massachusetts had received word that his nephew, a Navy SEAL who had volunteered for the Coalition Fleet, had died on this far off world under mysterious circumstances. Captain Brooks apparently had a brother still out there somewhere, fighting.

The Senator loved his sister, and she loved her sons. The Brooks family was wealthy and powerful with a proud history of military service going all the way back to the Civil War. Mama Brooks had been furious when her sons volunteered for the Coalition Fleet. And now, with one still out there somewhere, and one dead under mysterious circumstances...well, she wanted answers.

And she was willing to pay to get them. Pay. Threaten. Cajole. Demand. She was willing to hurt my son to discover the truth about hers. I understood a mother's love, the relentless ache of it. I'd agreed to take this assignment, not because I wanted to, but because refusing would cause Wyatt more pain. Success, however, would see his surgery paid for and performed by the very best doctors the Brooks family could afford.

And they could afford a lot.

And all I had to do was bring them the truth about the prison colony. The contaminated flesh of our warriors. The truth about what was happening to our military personnel.

Captain Brooks had served his country well, then volunteered to go into space as a Coalition fighter and battle the mysterious enemy no one had ever seen. The Hive. Rumors and conspiracy theories were everywhere. But these creatures were supposed to be terrifying beings straight out of *Star Trek*. Monsters so scary that the governments of Earth had agreed to the Coalition demand for brides and warriors to protect us from a Hive invasion.

A lot of people didn't believe the Hive existed. That the whole thing was a government conspiracy, a cover-up, a way to sacrifice people to some strange alien force without raising alarm. Some thought our volunteers were nothing more than cattle being led to slaughter. The information shared on the news networks was vague. No pictures of these Hive were ever shared. They were just bad guys in space, far away, mythical things that could never hurt us. But that seemed to be just what the governments wanted us to know. People in power argued that if the truth of what was outside of our atmosphere, beyond our moon and the reaches of our space shuttles was shared, there would be pandemonium. Riots. Chaos in the streets.

They wanted to the truth to remain hidden, it seemed, for our own good.

I didn't care about any of that. I cared about Wyatt and my mom. If someone was willing to pay me money to get the truth, then I'd go. I wasn't interested in the truth. I didn't care about conspiracy theories or cover-ups. I was interested in the money this assignment would pay. The surgery Wyatt needed that this money would cover. I cared about healing my son.

And if I failed? Well, there was a price to be paid. They would hurt him. They would kill my mother and torture my boy. Those small details something they'd chosen not to share with me until the very end, of course.

But I believed the threat. Something in Mrs. Brooks' fanatical gaze sent a shiver down my spine. She'd lost both of her sons and, apparently, her mind and sense of human decency. Too late to turn back now. The *only* thing I could focus on was getting back home to Wyatt, who was probably asleep under his Power Rangers comforter with a stuffed tiger named Roar snuggled under his sweet, innocent little chin at this very moment.

Space aliens weren't my biggest fear. Wyatt not being able to walk normally, not grow, be forced to watch from the sidelines as the other boys run and play? That would break his little heart, and my baby hurting was not acceptable. Not to me.

And the threats made against him? I couldn't bare to think about that. I simply would not fail.

I startled as the crate shifted under me and I realized it

was moving, swinging a bit as if being lifted and carried through the air on the end of a crane.

Everything was happening exactly as they'd told me it would.

Two days on board the freighter, arrival at the Colony. We'd landed a few hours ago, the rumble of the ship's engines nearly rattling my teeth out of my head as we'd landed. A slight jolt when it made contact with the planet's surface. And now, a few hours later, I was being off-loaded, stacked in their new storage facilities. I was packed in with a shipment of seeds from the Salvard Global Seed Vault. I'd been staring at their logo for so long, I could draw it in my sleep.

Apparently, the Colony was working to terraform their new planet to make it more appealing. They were bringing in plants native to every Coalition home world. I'd been sleeping next to thirty-foot tall maple, elm and locust trees. Also in the hold were spruce and drought resistant shrubs of every variety. Huge trees, too big to send via their precious transport technology.

We were headed to Base 3, where the Governor had, according to my sources, recently been mated through the Interstellar Brides Program to a woman from Earth. All of this was for her, his devotion—or obsession, depending on who told the story—was so complete that he was creating an Earth garden just for her. I would be able to sneak onto the planet because of some woman named Rachel that I'd never met.

The ways onto the planet were limited. No one from Earth was allowed unless he or she was a Coalition fighter or a bride. I wasn't the military type. I'd never even held a gun before. The other option was to volunteer for the Interstellar Brides Program, but I didn't meet their requirements. I had Wyatt. I was a mother. Besides, I had zero interest in being a mate of a space alien, or in leaving Earth.

No. I just wanted to get the damn story and get home. And so I was being drop shipped with a bunch of Earth trees as if by FedEx.

How this was possible on a prison planet, I wasn't sure. But then, that was the reason for my assignment. To discover the truth about The Colony. To expose it. To get word back to Earth about what was really going on here. The shipment really was of trees and shrubs, flowers and bulbs. There weren't military-grade arms hidden away. I'd had two long travel days to have proof of that. So was the shipment really because a governor on the planet loved his Earth mate? If that was the case, why had I been dressed in armor and warned to avoid detection at all costs? This damn suit of armor recorded everything, every heartbeat and blink of my eye, every second of activity, everything I heard or saw. If it so dangerous on the prison planet, why the trees?

Didn't matter. *Didn't matter. Get in, get the info. Get home to Wyatt.*

Shit. The armor. Stupid people back on Earth would probably download the data from it and wonder why the hell I'd just had an orgasm. I hoped not. Please, no. There were some details better left alone.

Dreaming about hunky Greek gods shoving me up against a wall and making me scream? Yep. That was one of those private kinds of things.

The crate settled with a soft bang and I checked the timer. I was to wait exactly twenty minutes, use the tools they'd given me to remove the bolts, remove the side panel, replace it, and find somewhere to hide and observe. I was supposed to remain hidden and gather information. That's it. I had to be back here, back inside the crate in three days for the trip home. I checked my wrist unit and sighed with relief when I saw the counter was functional. Seventy hours and five minutes until I got to go home.

I had a map of the base, but they'd warned me not to trust it. The information was at least five months old and things move. They change. Empty rooms might not be empty.

But I was sneaky, and small, and quick. I'd been a gymnast in high school. I could scale walls and hang from rafters if I needed to.

When the time showed twenty minutes and two seconds, I took two deep breaths and put on my helmet before lifting the small drill to the corners of the crate and getting to work. To say I was eager to get out of the crate was an understatement. I'd never been claustrophobic before, but I was ready for some fresh air, some windows even.

Five minutes later I was free, the side replaced. I took deep breaths to calm my racing heart. God, I was really doing this. I looked around. The main lights were off in the storage room, only a few emergency beacons gave the space a soft white glow. Every crate and tree were giant shadows looming above me.

I was alone on an alien world, but I felt hunted. Watched.

Even the trees seemed to be keeping an eye on me.

Shrugging off the feeling, I scurried like a mouse to the edge of the storage room and started looking for the vents. The map I had memorized detailed a large air control system, the vents big enough for me to walk upright. The system of air tunnels formed a maze beneath the base. I tried not to think about going from one small space to another. I took a deep breath and thought about my son.

He didn't need a weak, frightened mother. He needed me, he needed me to be strong.

And like the proverbial rat, I entered the maze. I had no choice but to try to survive it.

CHAPTER 2

K iel, *Everian Hunter, The Colony*

THE TIGHT, wet walls of her pussy clenched down on my cock. I tried to be gentle, to hold back, but it hadn't worked. Not when her soft voice all but begged me to fuck her. She wanted my cock, wanted it to fill her up. I wasn't going to deny her, or myself, that pleasure.

I wasn't one to let a female tell me what to do. I was the one in control. I was the powerful one. I was the protector, guardian, dominant. But when her pussy dripped all over my cock head, she had all the power and I all but bowed down to her. And when I was buried balls deep and my orgasm was building at the base of my spine, I'd given up. I took her. Hard. Deep. With masterful strokes, I brought her to the brink and then over. It was the sharp bite of her fingernails digging into my shoulders that pushed me over the edge. The feel of her heels pressing against my ass, pulling me into her impossibly deeper. The sound of her voice as she screamed her pleasure.

But it was the roar of my own release that woke me to my empty room. There was no woman pressed against a wall. No woman I held in place, her body settled onto my hard length, taking all of me, milking me deep. I was alone in my bed and I'd just come all over myself. My fist was wrapped around my throbbing member, seed still pulsing from the tip. There was so much. Too much. I had no memory of coming this hard before, and there was no willing female begging me to fuck her. No scent of her. Nothing. Nothing but a lingering dream and a body spun so tightly I felt like I was about to burst out of my skin.

My breathing was ragged, my skin heated. The simple sheet over me was too much. I pushed it down, felt the hot smear of my cum on my thighs. I closed my eyes, savored the last remnants of the mind-blowing orgasm. I exhaled deeply, gave over to the post-coital lethargy, but there'd been no fucking. No, I had a wet dream like a horny teenager. I hadn't been able to control my impulses, my needs. It had been out of my control.

I stroked myself, working the last drops of seed from the tip. My belly was coated in the white essence and it began to cool.

"Fuck." What the *fuck* had just happened? Had the Hive managed to get inside my head? Had they fucked with my mind the same way they'd fucked with my body?

All the hours they'd spent trying to force me to breed for them, to give them my seed, to fuck their disturbing female drones, I'd endured.

And now? One look at *her*, Lindsey, and I'd faltered. Lost my will to resist. To fight.

It had to be a trap, a trick of the mind. There were no

women on the Colony who looked like her. No unclaimed females wandering the halls at night, passing so close that I might recognize the call of a marked mate and dream share with her.

This was the cruelest trick yet, not because the dream wasn't pleasant, but because it had broken me. Bent me to their will—no—to *her* will.

Grabbing the sheet, I wiped my hand, then the rest of me. My skin was damp not only from my spilled emission, but from sweat. The dream had been hot. Heavy. My cock hadn't diminished. It was still hard, still primed to fuck again.

To fuck *her.*

Her.

My mate.

I sat up then, drew my knees in, my eager cock pressing against my belly. It was the sure sign that what my mind was telling me was true. My cock knew.

My mate was near. Near enough to dream share.

I looked down at the palm of my hand, expecting to see nothing. Instead, I barely dared to breathe as I studied the hot, red mark that had been dormant my entire life. The birthmark of the Everian bloodlines burned. Tingled. Awake.

But that was impossible.

Even as I thought the word, my body disagreed. *Mate.*

Lindsey. My mate was Lindsey and she had gorgeous pale hair. So soft between my fingers. Her body was perfect, her hips wide and lush, my hands sank into her soft flesh as I held her up, held her in place as I fucked her deep. Her nipples were hard points, firm and hot against the roof of my mouth. Her cries of pleasure still echoed in my head.

Lindsey.

It had to be wrong. There was no mate for me here. No mate would be on The Colony. Those of us doomed to live here were banished, exiled. Left to a life alone. No mate, no family. Nothing but the memories of fighting and torture by the Hive. Nothing but barren, rugged landscape and a heart that matched.

But now? The pleasure lingered. My cock pulsed ready to fuck again. I *had* fucked her. I felt her, heard her. Shared with her.

I grabbed my hand, rubbed my thumb over the mark that was now hot, pulsing. Awakened for the first time.

But how?

Everian mates dream shared when their marked mate was near. I was old, too old to have hope left of finding my marked mate. It was hard when on Everis; not all marked mates found each other. But here, on The Colony? Impossible. There were no females here except the few who had been matched through the Brides Program. The few who had been Coalition fighters and escaped the atrocities of the Hive. They were settled on Base 6, on the other side of the planet. They'd been here long enough that if we were fated, then my mark would have awakened long before now. No, they were not for me.

But Lindsey was.

I swung my legs over the side of the bed, let the air dry my damp skin. I ran my hand through my hair, took deep breaths to still my heart, but nothing would still my racing thoughts.

My mate was here. On The Colony. She had to be to be within the area of proximity for my mark to awaken, for us to dream share. She was nearby. Somewhere. Close enough to meet her in my dreams, to know she was perfect. I wanted her. So did my cock.

I gripped the base, stroked it, my thumb sliding over the underside of the head. I had to come again. The need for her was too great. I didn't know anything about her, except I knew what she looked like, what she felt like when I was buried deep inside her, what she sounded like when she came.

Fuck, I was going to come, and only after a few strokes. If I didn't remember the dream, I'd think something was wrong with me. Did other Everian males behave this way when they found their mate? Did they come all over themselves? Not once, but twice?

Fuck. I spurted hotly all over my hand, the sharp pleasure made me grit my teeth. I caught my breath. Again. I wiped my cum away. Again.

I stood, looked down at my cock.

Still hard. Still fucking needy for her pussy. The vein pulsed along the side, the head almost purple, angry that it could not be sated.

A beep came from the comm unit. I ran a hand over my face, felt the rasp of my whiskers. I walked to the table, picked up my wrist unit.

"Hunter Kiel," I said, my voice harsh. Shit. Was this what the dream was doing to me?

"Kiel. We have a security breach."

It was Governor Rone. Fortunately, if he noticed my gruff tone, he hadn't mentioned it. He wasn't one for many words when only a few would suffice. We were similar in that and perhaps that was why I respected the Prillon warrior so much. He also wouldn't have called me for a petty task so this had to be serious.

The usual sharp awareness that filled me the moment I heard a message like this, one specifically tied to my hunting skills, pushed against the aftereffects of my dream, but could not take control. No, the mark was too powerful. I stood naked, cock hard, my need still thrumming through my veins

21

and tried to think through the fog of lust clouding my mind, the fog of *her*.

The governor of our base called upon me to be the Hunter I was. That was my value to this planet. But my need? The intense pull the mark now had on me? It was for a different hunt entirely. I had to find her, to find my marked mate, wherever the hell she was, on this planet or another.

And what was that strange room in her dream? The small child in the strange, metal walled bed? The older woman sleeping slumped in a chair? Was that her home? Was that where I would find her? *Lindsey.*

"Hunter Kiel," the Governor Rone repeated, breaking my thoughts. My mark burned, reminding me of my priorities. Finding *her* was my personal mission now, but I also worked for the governor and for every warrior who was trapped on this planet with me. The Hive had caused trouble here the last few weeks, infiltrating our sanctuary—or our prison—depending on one's point of view. The Hive had turned The Colony into a dangerous, uncertain place. The guarded looks the warriors here gave one another, the fear they tried to hide—fear that the Hive would once more have control of their minds, their bodies—the thought made me shudder as well. I was born to fear nothing, but even I could not deny the tremor that raced through me at the thought of being captured once more.

Tortured.

Changed.

The only way to control the fear was to hunt. And hunting the Hive was my specialty.

"Kiel? Can you hear me?"

"Yes, Maxim. I will come to the command center directly," I replied.

"Hurry," he replied, ending the communication.

I went to the S-Gen unit in the corner and stood on the black scanning pad. The thin green lights activated as the Spontaneous Matter Generator created fresh armor and weapon for me. The armor was standard Coalition, the mottled black and grey a fitting camouflage for most expeditions in deep space. The ion blaster was small and I strapped it to my thigh. The armor was light and comfortable. Some warriors on the base had begun to wear civilian clothing once more, colors and soft, flowing fabrics in designs common on the various home worlds now brightened the main areas and dining hall.

The brides had done that, brought a touch of normalcy to a situation that was anything but. I, however, felt naked and exposed without my armor, as did many of the others. And with a traitor still loose and the Hive building secret, underground operating stations in caves, I needed to hunt, not sit, chat and sip wine with the women like a trained pet.

Groaning, I shifted things around in my pants. Apparently, I was going to have a meeting with the security team and the governor of Base 3 with a hard on. My desire had not waned and my cock wasn't going to stand down, no matter the topic. I had to hope the armor shielded the obvious. My mark had been awakened and nothing was going to ease me except finding and claiming my mate.

"THERE." The governor, Maxim, pointed at the vid screen. I followed his finger and saw the intruder. The image was crystal clear, crisp. The male wore the usual armor of a Coalition fighter; pants, shirt, even the helmet, and moved with the lithe ease of an athlete and the surety of one who knew exactly where to go as he removed a grate and disappeared inside the ventilation tunnels that ran beneath the entire base.

"How long ago was this taken?" I asked. Maxim and I stood side-by-side. I rivaled him for height, but I was less bulky than the Prillon, allowing me to move swiftly on a hunt. I was dexterous and nimble, yet it took hard work and constant training to remain in top form.

"Twenty minutes." The governor was a powerful warrior; he now served The Colony with his leadership skills. He'd been chosen, elected by the warriors who would answer to him. There was no higher honor among warriors and I respected that. He served as the Colony's liaison to the Brides Processing Center on Earth and had been mated, with his second, Ryston, to a brilliant human scientist with dark hair and a stubborn slant to her eyes that I admired. Together, their bond had lit the spark of hope through the Colony. They appeared together in public often, trying to inspire the others to hope, to dream, to submit to the mental invasion of the Interstellar Brides Processing protocols. Many had and waited for a match.

I was Maxim's opposite, my strengths sending me out to hunt in the shadows. Unseen. Deadly.

Not exactly inspiring. Seeing me usually inspired fear, not hope. No matter that I'd picked up a team of sorts including the human hunter, a bride named Kristin, who'd arrived to mate the Prillon warriors Tyran and Hunt. Also in the group, a Prillon warrior named Marz who'd become one of the few males I trusted during our time with the Hive. Lastly, a big, pain-in-my-ass Atlan Warlord with a temper to match. Rezzer. He fought his beast every fucking day. And every day, I wondered if I'd be called upon to terminate a friend.

"Has he been picked up by the other surveillance nearby?" I asked. The surveillance in the storage area had caught the heat shift of a living being and set off the warning sensors.

"Negative," one of the security team said. He sat before the controls, his fingers sliding over the glossy panel as his eyes followed the results on the various vid screens before us. The entire wall was of different images from around Base 3. At first it was difficult to process, so many places to monitor and observe, but I recognized it was an organized system. The screens were arranged north to south, east to west geographically throughout the Base.

The tech, a warrior from the planet Trion, frowned. "The first warning signal came twenty minutes ago and from within the storage area. No sensors have picked him up in the corridors or anywhere else before that."

"He had to come from somewhere," the governor added, his voice a mixture of genuine surprise and a hint of frustration. He glanced down at the security tech, then back up at the display.

"There is no data that shows he actually did come from somewhere. It's as if—" He didn't finish the words.

"He didn't transport in," I added, saying aloud what I knew to be true. One thing the Coalition did control with an unbreakable fist, was their transport technology. If you weren't authorized, you didn't go anywhere. Ever.

"No, he did not," the second security tech confirmed. "I've checked with the transport station. No transports in the last two days. In or out."

It was possible to transport onto the Base elsewhere besides the transport station with the correct coordinates, however the team would know, even if someone attempted it without appropriate approval. That kind of data was easily picked up and ensured the Hive weren't just popping in for a quick battle.

"Then he must be someone we know. Sabotage?"

I didn't want to consider the possibility of another traitor in our midst.

I watched the male move across the display, his pace quick as he went from behind a storage container and to the large air shaft on the west wall. His helmet-covered head moved left and right as if scanning the area, but nothing slowed him down. He even knew where to wave his hand on the wall to have the access panel open.

My mark flared, pulsed with a heat that almost burned as I watched the recording. I rubbed the spot, but it didn't lessen.

"Why would he bother going into the air shaft?" the governor asked. "The entire system is automated and controlled from elsewhere. Even if he wanted to poison the air, or gas us in our sleep, it would be impossible." He turned to me, his shrewd gaze meeting mine as I looked away from the display. The pulsing in my hand lessened. "There's no fucking reason for anyone to be in there."

Looking back at the male who was the latest mystery on our struggling planet, my mark flared again. "Except to hide."

"What?"

"I'll find him," I muttered under my breath. Why was my mark responding to the image of a male on a vid screen? There had to be something wrong with me, for my cock pressed against the heavy armor. While some males might be attracted to other males, I wasn't. I got hard thinking of a female's perfect curves, the soft feel of her breasts in my palms, the wet heat of her pussy. I wanted a mate. A *female* mate. I wanted Lindsey. After the dream we just shared, only her. My mark would want no one else.

So why the fuck was I eager to go after the bastard in the air shaft? Was my lust for a mate increasing my need to hunt?

Perhaps I was succumbing to whatever the traitor, Krael Gerton, had brought to the planet. He'd worked with the Hive to destroy us all. Prior to my arrival, his frequency generator had reactivated some Hive implants. Combined with Quell injections, he'd murdered one man from Earth and nearly killed Governor Maxim.

The Governor's new mate, a brilliant scientist named Rachel, had figured out his plan and stopped him, but he'd slipped through their fingers.

But that was before me. I'd seen the traitor in the underground Hive Integration station here on the Colony. I'd wanted to rip him into pieces.

He'd escaped. He'd killed my friend, Marz's second, the Prillon Captain Perro. Since then, I'd hunted him. Twice we'd had him cornered in the caverns that formed an endless system of natural tunnels and caves beneath the surface. And both times, he'd escaped me.

Not that it mattered. I hunted. It was who I was born to be. And his scent, the rhythm of his heartbeat called to me through the thickest rock, across time and space with a knowing that I could not explain but didn't question. The traitor would die. I would see to it personally.

I wasn't affected as Captain Brooks had been. I was not vulnerable to Hive transmissions, as some were. Hell, I barely had any cyborg parts. The one implant in my left arm so small it had no effect on my body or abilities. But it had been their mark of ownership, their attempt to control me. Enough to earn me banishment here, just like the rest of the castoffs and rejected warriors.

I didn't have Black Death creeping under my skin or Hive commands buzzing around inside my mind. No, I had a cock stand that could break rocks and a mark that burned for my one true mate. But there was no mate. Lindsey was only in my dreams.

Had the Hive finally broken my mind? All their torture and torment had been designed to force me to impregnate their strange drone females. But Hunter DNA was strong, and seemed to have a knowing all its own. There was no forcing a Hunter to breed. It was, literally, impossible. Stolen seed would die, the progeny never take root in a female womb.

But with Lindsey? Gods, I'd fuck her three times a day to see my seed take root and grow. The urge to fill her with my child was violent and undeniable.

My mate. How the fuck was I dream sharing with a female when there were no unmated women on the entire planet?

I'd gone mad.

"Hunter? You with me?" The Governor's arms were crossed and his brow furrowed. He tapped his foot in a rare outward sign of annoyance.

Why was I here? Oh, yes. An intruder. "Yes. I'm here." As much as I could be with the memory of Lindsey's hot pussy milking me dry still spinning in my mind.

"Find the intruder quickly," the governor commanded. "Find out what the fuck he's doing. If he's an enemy, if he's working with the traitor, I want him dead by nightfall."

I nodded to the governor. After all the shit that had been happening on The Colony—death, Hive infiltration, treason—we didn't need more.

When the traitor had been one of us, he'd had many friends. But now, his name was not spoken, at least not by any who lived and breathed on the Colony. He was simply, *the traitor.*

I was new here, but I was settling in and considered The Colony my home. I wanted the traitor found as much as the governor and it was my job to find him and mete out justice. I was a Hunter. Vengeance was in my very blood.

If this mystery intruder was going to kill us all, I could hunt him despite my painful need to fuck and a burning mark. That—or whatever was wrong with me—would have to wait. *Lindsey* would have to wait. Even if I could find her, I would not bring a new mate here under such a threat.

I slapped a hand on the top of the control panel, the sound spurring me into action, the painful strike redirecting my mind off my mark. "Get me the plans for the ventilation tunnels. I'll find him."

CHAPTER 3

$\mathcal{L}$ indsey

I FOLLOWED the sound of voices, shouting, cheers through the vast network of Base 3's air shafts. While I'd been given a map showing the spider web path they took, they hadn't told me the air kicked on every few minutes or that I would be caught up in a hurricane. At first, I'd panicked, thinking I was going to be knocked off my feet and pushed through the tunnel like a tumbleweed across an open prairie. I'd put my hand up on the smooth metal, but there was nothing to grab and hold on to, so I'd dropped to my knees, tucked my head down and waited. It lasted perhaps thirty seconds, then stopped as abruptly as it had begun.

Once it was quiet again, only the lingering roar in my ears remained, I took a few deep breaths, savored the stillness, then continued on. I was supposed to go to the command center first—the heart of the operation within this specific Base—but the consistent blasts of air every few minutes had me wanting out of the super-sized shafts.

Yes, I was hidden in here. Yes, it was an easy way to get out of the storage area unseen. But those were the only positives. If I hadn't worn my helmet, I would have had no protection for my eyes. The air blew so strongly I wasn't sure I'd be able to suck in a breath with my face bare. And I could only imagine what my hair would have looked like. I never went in for the whole "windblown look." I made that mistake exactly once, getting on the back of my high school boyfriend's motorcycle with my long blond hair flying, whipping behind me like a banner shouting my wild, reckless freedom.

It had been wonderful. Liberating. Exhilarating. I felt like a movie star or a shooting comet. Until we stopped.

Three hours. It had taken my mother three hours, two hair washings and half a bottle of conditioner to untangle the mess and I'd never done it again.

I learned. Eventually. Usually, I learned life's lessons the hard way—but I did learn.

When I heard the voices, the shouts, I was drawn to the noise. Yes, I was on a mission, but I was the only one here from Earth investigating a strange planet from an air shaft. Everyone else was light years away getting Big Macs from McDonalds and sleeping in their own beds. If I wanted to deviate a little bit, so be it. And besides, I was supposed to find men from Earth, Navy SEALS and soldiers and marines locked away like prisoners. I wasn't going to see anything interesting crawling around these stupid air tunnels.

Resolved, and curious, I followed the sounds of people— of aliens—instead of going to the central part of the Base. I'd been asked to find out what was happening on The Colony, right? And the only way to do that was to watch the inhabitants, and by the sound of it, quite a number of them were directly ahead.

Why were they so loud? So excited? Judging by the way the shouts bounced and echoed through the cavernous tunnels and the metal walls, it was a large group and they were doing something. Watching something that ebbed and flowed. Like a contest of some kind.

Or an MMA fight.

I literally saw light at the end of the tunnel. White strips of it cut through the vent opening. Leaning against the wall, I angled my head so I could look through.

This was it. The moment I saw aliens for the first time. Would they be green and have scales like a lizard? Would they be blue tinged and have weird gills? Tails? Two heads? An eye in the center of their forehead or a forked tongue?

God, what if they wanted to eat me?

No. No! That wasn't possible. The go-team would have warned me of that, wouldn't they? And besides, if humans were food, there wouldn't be human fighters walking around for me to film. Right?

Right?

The air vortex kicked on again and I crouched down, counted to thirty in my head. I was pretty close and it shut off at twenty-eight.

Enough. I couldn't stand it any longer, so I peeked out, took my first look at The Colony.

Stretched out below me was some kind of amphitheater and it was filled with men. No, not men. Aliens. Really *big* aliens.

I could only see their backs as they were all looking down at something. I couldn't see what it was they were shouting, jeering and cheering at because they were all so damn big. Broad shouldered and tall, not quite giants, but bigger than most men on Earth except perhaps the defensive line for the Chicago Bears. Most of them wore armor similar to mine, but sized to fit their huge physiques perfectly. At least my handlers at home had been right about the wardrobe.

They weren't green. Or blue. From here, they looked like men from Earth, only much, much bigger. Brown hair. Golden. Black. A beautiful, copper red.

I sighed, a bit disappointed, if I was being perfectly honest. Where were the blue skinned barbarians I loved reading about in one of my favorite romance series? Where were the guys with scales who could shape-shift into dragons and breathe mating fire into a woman's body and make her burn with desire?

Brown freaking hair? Really?

I hadn't seen their faces yet, but they all had two arms, two legs, very nicely shaped asses and massive, panty-melting shoulders.

God, I loved a good set of shoulders.

Which made me think of Kiel, and that weird dream— that amazing, wonderful, wicked dream. Kiel, with his dark hair and eyes, and that big, orgasm inducing cock…

My hand flared with heat and my pussy clenched. Another burst of air came through and I dropped to my knees again. Crap. This was the fifth, maybe sixth, time it had happened. I tucked my head and counted, waited it out. I was so done with the damn air. The ducts. Small spaces. Two days locked in a crate, and now, my head crammed into this stupid helmet. The air stopped.

A round of cheers filled the air, everyone's focus was away from me, so I took the opportunity to open the latch and slip past the slatted door. Leaning against the stone wall, I looked around. The circular area was some kind of arena and cut out entirely from the rocky terrain. While I noticed the sky was blue and there were two moons, I knew I had to focus on all of the aliens, not the dang sky. I had the same outfit as they did. I was small, a lot smaller than most of them, but I could blend in. I just had to join the crowd, to participate. No one would know I wasn't from The Colony. I'd see what held their attention. It wasn't just a journalist's curiosity. I wanted to stay out of the damn air shaft.

I stepped closer to the aliens, but they were so broad, so tall, I couldn't see past them. I skirted around the upper tier, trying to find an opening. I made it halfway around and picked up some conversation.

"—the best on The Colony."

"I've never seen a fighter like him."

"Even Prillons can't take on an Atlan in beast mode."

"Together? I'm betting on the Prillons."

"Rezz will send them to medical."

"How many do you think he can take?"

I skirted the edges, clinging to the back wall, trying to stay in the shadows. No one paid any attention to me, their complete focus on the contest about to begin in the ring. The tension in the air was growing as anticipation made the men edgy and primed for competition, for violence.

My shoulder bumped into a large brace that curved up over my head. The giant piece of metal was at least three feet wide and curved up to connect to a series of overhead beams that supported a clear-domed roof at least thirty feet above my head. Each beam had a two or three inch ledge that I could use to climb, and once I was up there, they were wide enough that I could lay down on my stomach, watch everything and not be seen. Perfect.

If I could just make it up there.

With a grin, I adjusted the pack on my back and lifted my foot to the lower ledge. Years of gymnastics and messing around on the rock climbing wall at the local YMCA were paying off, big time, as I climbed up and hoisted myself onto the top of the beam. Crouched low, I climbed about a third of the way up, finally found a space, settled in on my belly and peered over the edge, looking down. Shit. It was the closest thing to a gladiator fight I could imagine. The arena was a full circle. Small, perhaps the size of a one-ring circus. In the center, the ground was dirt and two men stood facing a giant.

No, not men. The two fighting the giant faced my direction and they were *not* like any men I'd ever seen. They were aliens and the disappointment I'd been feeling just moments ago died. These two were obviously from the same planet, one a dark mocha, the other with pale golden skin and copper hair. Their faces weren't quite human either, their noses, eyes and chins too sharply pointed. Neither was less than six-six, but their eyes gave them away. Gold and copper. And when they smiled, they flashed a hint of fang, not enough to be vampirish, but enough to make me lean forward trying to get a closer look.

Fascinating.

Not human. Soooo not human. But damn. None of them wore a shirt and I'd never seen a more spectacular display of masculine beauty. Well, except for in my dream earlier, but that hardly counted. These were real, flesh and blood and standing right in front of me.

And the model perfect chests on the two challengers were small compared to the bulging muscles and massive frame of the giant they faced. He was monster sized, his profile oddly elongated, as if his face had grown out of proportion to the gigantic rest of him. He was even bigger than the other two, towering over his opponents whose heads barely reached the top of his shoulders. The men in the crowd were chanting, and the giant raised his hands in the air like a victor, rotating his torso to acknowledge the cheers. His knuckles were bloody and he had more blood running from a small cut near his eye, but he was *smiling*.

"Rezzer! Rezzer! Rezzer!"

Other than the fact that he was massive, he looked the most human of the bunch. My theories of lizards and blue skin were for nothing. No one, not one spectator, looked completely different from an Earth man. Some had different skin coloring, sharper features, but not enough to be alarming. Just odd. And huge. Big huge. Like...huge huge.

What I quickly noticed was that every single person in the crowd was a man. Scanning the crowd, I didn't see one woman, alien or not. I was the only female here. Strange. Where were the women?

The sound of a fist connecting with flesh and bone filled the air, followed by cheers and shouts. My curiosity quickly forgotten, I redirected my focus to the fighters as my pulse pounded in my ears and I fought to control my breathing inside the helmet. Below me, chests heaved and I could practically taste the testosterone in the air. It was like being inside the male mind, surrounded by heat and power and...rage.

The intensity of my reaction startled me as anger rose to choke me. I swallowed hard, fighting the burning sting that gathered behind my eyelids as the giant below me bellowed out a challenge that made the entire crowd roar. An answering yell exploded inside my chest, but I clenched my jaw and held it inside, locked away with the rest of the emotions I couldn't deal with right now.

I didn't want to be here, belly down, on this stupid beam twenty feet in the air on an alien planet. I didn't want to have one more nightmare about my beautiful, broken little boy and his innocent, trusting eyes. He was mine, and he believed me when I told him everything was going to be all right.

Everything had to be all right. I'd do whatever I had to do. For my son, I would lie, cheat, steal, fly halfway across the galaxy locked in a crate. For Wyatt, I would do anything, risk anything. Even my life. I was no killer. I wasn't a fighter or a soldier, but for Wyatt? I was a mother, and that meant nothing was out of bounds. Absolutely...nothing.

I blinked slowly, clearing the wetness from my eyes as the hot sting of tears tracked down my cheeks beneath the helmet. I couldn't wipe them away, so I ignored them and clung to the beam, my fingers tight with tension where my dark, gloved hands wrapped around the edges securing my perch.

Below, the darker-skinned of the two smaller challengers was gone. A quick scan of the ground showed him tossed aside and unconscious several feet outside the center fighting area. Two men wearing green uniforms were bent over him, running some kind of blue light over his body like a scanner straight out of a sci-fi movie.

Everyone ignored them, so I did, too, my gaze drawn like a magnet to the force and power at the center of the arena floor.

Two remained, circling each other, arms up, fists clenched. The lone challenger had pale caramel skin and copper-colored hair. The giant faced me now and I got my first good look at his features. He was handsome, despite his size, with dark hair and green eyes. His stare was intense, focused, but he had to be well over eight feet tall. His hands were like dinner plates and his muscles seemed to have their own muscles. They both wore the armored uniform, but their shirts had been discarded and left on the ground behind them. They were bare from the waist up and to say they were both hot was an understatement. My ovaries perked right up at the sight of their broad chests, wide shoulders, rippled abs.

The bigger one had a smattering of hair on his chest that tapered into a line that slipped beneath the waistband of his pants. Below was a very serious bulge. The other fighter wasn't lacking in that department either.

I was enthralled, hypnotized by the intensity, the power. This wasn't a boxing match. It wasn't WWF. It wasn't even MMA. They dodged and weaved, moved with a pace that made me squint and lean forward, trying to keep track of them.

They came together in a clash of fists and fury. I expected the smaller opponent to be tossed aside as quickly as his friend had been, but Rezzer, which I assumed was the giant's name, and the man were locked together, muscles bulging to the point of breaking. I winced at the force the two exerted on one another, waited for a shoulder joint to pop, or an elbow to break.

No one could withstand that kind of pressure. Locked together, they circled one another and suddenly the copper haired alien's back was to me. That's when I noticed the silver skin that covered half of his back and wrapped around his neck. The silver sparkled in the light like he'd been dusted with a thin coating of glitter. The arena lights were bright in the center of the ring, spotlights shone down on the fighters so there was nowhere to hide.

Hive. Cyborg. *Contaminated flesh.* The words floated through my mind from my conversations with the doctor back on Earth. The Colony was for warriors who had been implanted with Hive technology. That silver skin sealed his fate...all of their fates. This place was their end, their prison.

Men screamed and roared as the two below me moved faster than any living thing I'd seen before.

Suddenly, the spectacle below made me sick. The violence

made bile rise in my throat and I turned to rest the face of my helmet against the beam. I couldn't feel the cool metal on my face, but I pretended as I heard Rezzer bellow one final time. The crowd erupted in cheers three times louder than anything I'd heard before and I peeked back down to see that his final challenger was struggling to rise, blood running down his face, copper colored blood, too orange to be human.

His right arm hung at an odd angle and the green uniformed men rushed forward with their magic blue wand.

My palm chose that moment to pulse with heat, but I clenched my hand tighter on the beam and ignored it. Apparently, I'd been mesmerized by the testosterone coming off the fighters for my pussy clenched and a rush of desire heated my blood. Maybe it was a reaction to the fight. I had no idea, but I could do no more than lick my lips and ogle the abundance of man candy before me. I should blame my distraction on estrogen, but really, I had no idea what to do next. I scanned the crowd, looking for human men, but if any were here, they were hidden among the others, a sea of black armor and aggressive faces.

The mark pulsed again and I hissed in a breath as my nipples pebbled and my stomach clenched. It was like the dream all over again, except instead of staring into the eyes of the hottest damn man I'd ever seen, I clung to a beam, hiding from a sea of violent, alien fight mania. I'd seen this before, the mob mentality, the wave of aggression that everyone present would be riding for hours. I'd gone to exactly one MMA fight with the sperm donor, and that had been enough for me.

This was too much.

Trembling, I wasn't sure staying up here another moment was safe. My hands were cramping and my entire body shook with stress and adrenaline. If I didn't get my act together, I could easily fall and break my neck. Or worse.

I laid completely still for long minutes, eyes closed, head down and focused on my breathing. Just air. In. Out. Until I could feel my toes again and my ears stopped ringing. The crowd had settled, their sport for the day over. I looked down and the warriors were milling about, talking, laughing, hitting each other, doing their male bonding stuff. I had to assume the giant, Rezzer, had won.

Whatever. I needed to get the hell out of here before I lost my shit.

Moving slowly, I scooted back the way I'd come, counting on the dim lights around the edges of the arena to help keep me hidden. I had just dropped to my feet and taken two steps back toward the air vent when an alien appeared out of nowhere, bumped into me and looked my way. I still had on my helmet, but he did a double take and then stilled.

Predator still. And like the proverbial deer in the head-lights, I froze as he leaned toward me, took a deep breath in and filled his lungs with my scent.

"Female." His voice was deep and full of awe, as if I was some kind of mythical creature, a unicorn. Based on the lack of females in the area, perhaps I was.

He looked like the bigger fighter, the one called Rezzer, and I assumed they were from the same planet. Similar size, coloring and those dinner plate hands. The last, I felt, for he gripped my upper arm. While his hold was gentle, it was a vise locked about me. I tried to wiggle out, but he wasn't letting go. His strength was indisputable and I knew, without even blinking, he could snap me in half like a twig. Holy shit, these guys were big. I barely came to his shoulder.

"Female," he repeated and before my eyes, he grew, like the Incredible Hulk until my head barely reached his chest.

He'd been big before, but now he was monster sized, too, and a roar left his throat. "Mine!"

"Oh my god," I murmured, my heart practically stuttering in my chest. I would have fainted, but I couldn't even do that. I was literally frozen in place, but my hand burned like fire and I suddenly wished I was back in the air shaft. No, back sleeping with my strange dream man, rather than facing down a mob of horny aliens. Insanely, I wasn't worried about being raped. I had the distinct feeling Mr. Dinner Plate wouldn't let anyone else touch me.

No. Right now, he was the one I needed to worry about.

The man's—no alien's—voice was loud, loud enough where those around us turned and came closer.

I was surrounded by looming, hot, aliens. Heard the murmurs of their voices at finding a female among them.

I felt the helmet come off my head and once it was gone, I twisted to look over my shoulder. Another caramel skinned male tucked it beneath his arm as he stared at me, then lifted a hand to touch my hair. Not with malice, but awe.

"Hey!" I said, trying to step back, but it was no use. I was held in place by Mr. Dinner Plate whose gaze followed the movements of the stranger's hand through my long blond hair as he combed his fingers through the strands.

If this was a petting zoo, apparently, I was the main attraction. I heard someone shout, "Get the Governor down here now!" But I had no idea who the Governor was, nor did I care. Not at the moment. Right now, I just wanted to get out of this mess and make a run for it.

News of my arrival spread faster than gossip at a church supper. The arena had gone quiet and everything seemed to have stopped.

"Mine! I claimed her," Mr. Dinner Plate repeated. He lifted me in his arms and carried me down the stairs to the center of the arena where the warrior, Rezzer, stood, flexing

42

his hands into fists. His chest was heaving and his green gaze met mine with cold calculation.

Behind him, his former opponent rose from the ground spinning his arms around, feeling the shoulder as if testing it out. Completely healed.

Holy shit. Was that what the little blue wand thing was for? To heal? Maybe I didn't need to spy and write some stupid conspiracy laden exposé. Maybe I just needed to steal one of those blue magic wands and take it home to Wyatt.

Even as I had the thought, I realized the futility of that hope. Right this moment, the people who'd offered me this job were waiting and watching my mother and my son. If I didn't come back, they would hurt him, torture my baby, perhaps even kill him. The consequences of failure had been explained in great detail. It wasn't just about the money or the story, not anymore. I either gave them what they wanted, or they were going to hurt the only two people in the universe I cared about.

Failure was not an option. I'd do whatever I had to do to survive, to get back to them. Wyatt needed me. I had to be strong.

Twisting my head around to keep my sight on the green uniformed warriors who moved away from the arena, I ignored the hulk carrying me until he set me down gently on the edge of the fighting pit. He placed me there like delicate china and I had to admit, he might be big, but he was a gentleman. He leaned down and looked into my eyes, his gaze a dark, golden brown and sincere. "I am Warlord Braun. You are mine, now. I will protect you."

Some kind of order appeared to have taken hold as the crowd resumed their seats. There were a handful of warriors lined up along the far edge of the arena, facing Braun.

I glanced at Rezzer, who stood with his arms crossed over his chest a few feet away, a frown on his face. Braun completely ignored him, and me, as he turned to face everyone gathered. "I am Warlord Braun and I claim this female."

"No. She will be ours." One of the golden warriors stepped forward with a nearly identical twin at his side.

"Mine!" Another giant came forward, nearly as big as Rezzer, already huge, his face transformed. His roar was nearly as loud as Braun's.

Pandemonium ensued as two aliens behind the one who held my helmet began shoving and punching each other. Why they fought, I had no idea. It appeared Braun had few challengers. Based on his size, that was completely understandable.

Braun stepped forward and motioned to the two golden aliens. With a groan, I bit my lip and looked around. Not one, but three warriors were lined up directly behind me, shoulder to shoulder. And they weren't watching the fight, they were watching me.

No easy getaway there.

"This is insane," I shouted at all of them. "I don't belong to any of you." With a sigh, I turned back around to see the golden ones step forward. One of them, I saw now, had a face half metallic and a completely silver eye. It was unnerving and strange, but then, everyone here seemed to me marked in some way by the silver flesh.

Contaminated. Imprisoned.

I was screwed. I'd done everything wrong. I was supposed to remain hidden. That hadn't happened. I was supposed to remain unobtrusive. Yeah, I couldn't get any more visible, and I hadn't even been trying.

I was a terrible spy. The worst.

Now I had hot aliens fighting over me, one claiming I belonged to him. I should have been flattered or impressed. I should have been thrilled. Heck, what woman wouldn't want a bunch of ridiculously hot aliens all wanting to claim her?

Me. That's who. I didn't want a mate. Yeah, dream man Kiel had been hot as hell, but I had a little boy to get home to and three days to make it back onboard that shuttle before it left. I wasn't going to miss my ride home. I'd survive now, escape later.

It was the only option I could think of because I had no idea how I was going to get out of this.

CHAPTER 4

I HAD a set of warriors in the air shaft following the intruder's path. I led two others and took a route outside, narrowing down the exits he might take, hoping to cut him off. The directions coming through the comm had us heading in the direction of the fighting pit and I had to hope we'd get there before he blended in. The space held over a hundred warriors. It would be easy for him to get lost in the crowd. It wasn't just my Hunter senses that were guiding me. No. That was enough for the governor to request me personally and be able to find the intruder easily enough. I was also guided by my mark. For some reason, each step I took closer to the fights, my mark pulsed and became hotter. It was not something I could ignore.

Why the fuck was my mark drawing me? There were no females on The Colony besides the few who had been matched and mated. No unclaimed female warriors were on

Base 3. My mark would have awakened long before now if the area of proximity was enough for any one of them from the other Bases to be mine. I hadn't been on The Colony long, but the dreams had just started. That meant she was new. Newer here than even me. But how?

"No one is in the air shafts now. The exhaust expulsion occurred two minutes ago. Any heat signature the intruder left behind is long gone."

We stopped not far from the fighting pit. I could hear the shouting, the fighting from here. The other two warriors assisting with the search, Prillons, looked to me. They knew my skills, knew I could find the trail of someone or something where no one else could see. Or sense.

"Which opening did he use to escape?" I asked, my wrist lifted.

"The south side of the pit."

"Of course," I muttered, the most crowded area here. More scents to track. I turned to the Prillons and wished I had my normal team with me, but Captain Marz was being tested for the Interstellar Brides Program, Kristin was spending time with her mates, and Rezz? Well, I was pretty sure the Atlan was down in the pits blowing off some steam. "Let's go. I'll have to pick up his trail at the vent."

"What about the fights?" I was asked.

"The less distraction from us, the better. I don't want everyone to know we're hunting."

They both nodded and we moved quickly to the fights.

"What the fuck?" one of the Prillons said, stopping and putting his hand on the ion pistol in his thigh holster.

I stopped as well, not only because I was surprised by what I was seeing, but because my mark flared as if a blade had been shoved through my palm. The sensation so painful it made me hiss out a breath. Instead of readying for danger as the Prillons were with their hands on their weapons, I pressed my thumb against my mark in the hopes of easing the burn.

"This is insane! I don't belong to you," a woman shouted.

I heard the feminine, melodious voice and I was forever changed. It was as if the ions in my body rearranged and I became someone else. My mark flared with erotic heat, sending a pulse of lust straight to my cock. My heart flipped, then settled. I felt as if those uttered words settled over me like a heavy cloak wrapping me in heat. Lust. Need. An instinctive drive to possess and protect.

Lindsey. She was here. She was mine.

My mate.

And then, with the same swiftness that brought about this knowledge, I picked up the scene before us. The two fighters —one of them was Rezz, my Atlan friend who had arrived on the Colony the same day as me. The other, I didn't know, but he was Atlan as well. With sweat on his face and torso, red skin in spots where blows had landed, blood trickling from a cut above his eye, it looked like Rezz had been fighting challenge matches for a while. But no one was battling now. No, they weren't even circling each other. Rezz was facing another Atlan and two Prillon warriors. Everyone else around the arena settled in with a quiet expectancy not common in a pit fight. This was something else, something much more serious than the normal chest pounding tests of strength and skill that the warriors used to vent some aggression and relieve hours of monotonous boredom.

I could see pushing and heard raised voices and somehow I knew she was in the middle of it. The cause.

I didn't need to be a Hunter to know where she was.

"She is mine." The huge Atlan facing Rezz was in full beast mode, and I recognized him now. His name was Braun, and he was strong. Fast. Like all Atlan Warlords.

I didn't fucking care how many of these warriors I had to

take down, Braun was wrong. Lindsey didn't belong to him. Lindsey, with her golden hair and blue eyes, those full pink lips and her sassy mouth...was mine.

I stalked forward, heading for the center of the pit, not waiting to see if my team backed me up. I didn't need them. Not for this. Anticipation surged through my blood. I hadn't had a real fight, a good fight, in weeks. Not even the Atlans could stand against me as long as I stayed out of their grasp. If one got ahold of me, they could rip me in two. But first, they'd have to catch me. Which, when I used my Hunter's speed and strength, was damn near impossible.

Pushing through the growing crowd I heard her again. "This is not what I wanted. Just take me to your leader, or whatever. I'm sorry."

Rezz, equal in size to Braun, roared out over the crowd. "The female is under my protection. None of you will touch her."

I knew Rezz, knew he'd never touch her. He was still too broken. He'd refused to go through the Interstellar Brides processing protocols even after Kristin arrived from Earth and became part of our hunting unit. The two human females who had arrived on the Colony loved their mates, despite the contamination the Hive had left behind. Captain Marz had practically begged the Atlan to submit to testing.

Rezz refused. Said he was not fit to serve any female of worth. Whatever the fuck that was supposed to mean.

I didn't care about Rezz's personal demons at the moment. All I knew was my friend had stepped between Braun, the two Prillon warriors, and the female who was mine. He was protecting her, a fact that I would not forget. Seemed I would owe the Atlan a favor.

"Get out of my way, Rezz." The deep, growling voice belonged to Braun but I heard Rezz chuckle in response. By the gods, that Warlord loved to fight.

"As I said, she's under my protection, Braun."

Braun roared in frustration, but must have decided that the small female wasn't worth the clash with Rezz, who was well known for being king in the pits since his arrival. Even Tyran, Kristin's mate, couldn't stand against him. And Tyran had more Hive implanted technology than almost any male here. He was stronger than anyone I'd ever seen.

Anyone but Rezz, riled up in beast mode. Still, the fight between Tyran and Rezz had been epic. In the end, I was convinced Rezz won not because the Prillon warrior was weaker, but because Rezz was meaner, especially since the male, Tyran, had been mated to the human, Kristin, of Earth. A small, curvy female that looked similar to Lindsey. Golden hair. Heart shaped face. So small, so damn small but fierce. I couldn't wait to discover what type of fire burned in Lindsey's delicate frame.

'Stop talking and get naked.'

The memory of the sensual demands she'd made in the dream riled me further and I rolled my head on my neck to ease the tension, to remain in control. Mine. She was mine. That voice was mine. Her body was mine. Her pleasure was mine. Her heart was mine. I never thought I'd take a mate, had given up on the idea the moment I'd been sentenced to life here, on this gods forsaken planet we all pretended wasn't a prison.

But now? She was here, and I'd rather die than give her up.

Braun leaped out of the middle of the pit to take a seat in the crowd, which left Rezz standing to face the two Prillon warriors. I cleared the edge of the arena just as Rezz stepped forward to stare down the two Prillons.

"Move aside, Rezz. We all know you don't want a mate." The larger of the two Prillons spoke, Captain Voth, his second nearly growling in agreement beside him.

51

Rezz pounded his right fist into the flat of his left palm and the sound was loud. Threatening. "You two want to spend the next twelve hours in a ReGen pod, that's all right with me."

"Please, don't. This is crazy."

I saw her then, for the first time. Yes, I'd seen her in the dreams, but I'd know her anywhere. As she spoke, she tried to hop down off the edge of the pit wall where she sat wearing standard issue Coalition battle armor. Her hair fell around her shoulders in a golden halo, more beautiful than even in the dream. Big green eyes stared out from a heart-shaped face that was too delicate to be real.

She tried to move, but two of the warriors standing directly behind her placed their hands on her shoulders to hold her in place.

I didn't recognize the growl that rose from my throat, but my Hunter took over.

Her soft cry sounded as I moved faster than a blur to shove the three men at her back away from her.

Rezz turned around to look up at where I now stood behind her, towering over her small frame. Her scent drifted up to me and my cock hardened instantly at the sweet scent of flowers and honey. This I'd missed in the dream. I wanted nothing more than to toss her over my shoulder and carry her back to my rooms, but I knew I'd never get her out of here without fighting at least one challenge.

"Kiel." Rezz's deep voice was like a crack of thunder through the arena and Lindsey gasped, her head whipping around to face me. But I didn't dare look down into those blue eyes. If I looked, I'd want to touch, and taste. And fuck.

"Warlord." I hopped over the side of the chest-high wall and into the pit, landing silently on my feet. I moved to my right, keeping both Rezz and the two Prillon who hadn't backed away in my sights. "Her name is Lindsey and she's mine. My marked mate."

A collective grumble rolled through the spectators as Rezz looked from me to the Prillon warriors who stood primed and ready for battle. His grin was amused, but he nodded to me before turning and looking at my mate. "Do you know this warrior, female?"

Lindsey's bright blue eyes flashed to me and she blushed, her cheeks turning a delicate and beautiful shade of pink. The way she gazed at me had my cock pulsing. Throbbing. My fingers itched to grab her. Touch her. Kiss her. Taste her for real. I'd never *needed* anything, but in that moment, I needed her.

"I've....I don't..." she stumbled over her words looking from me to Rezz and back again. I stepped forward, only too eager to remind her of our last encounter, but there was no need. Her gaze locked on me and I saw desire cloud her gaze. She looked me over, taking her time, inspecting every inch of me and I stood tall, thrilled as her breathing sped and her attention lingered. She was devouring me with her gaze, caressing me with her attention. Yes. She was mine.

I feared she would lie, deny me in front of all those gathered here. The air in my lungs stilled, even my heart seemed to stop beating as I waited for either salvation or rejection. It shouldn't matter. I hadn't even met her, not really. I'd only shared one dream with her. One. And suddenly I was terrified that wouldn't be enough. If she refused me now, something in me would break, something that, until this moment, I hadn't known existed. A soul? Love? I didn't know, but it was deep and instinctive. The Hunter in me was vulnerable to her in a way I'd never imagined possible. I was bare, exposed. Weak.

Everything in me teetered on the razor's edge as I willed her to save me. To claim me. To *want* me as badly as I wanted her. She licked her lips slowly, her eyes going soft as she studied my face as if shocked that I was real. Gods knew, I was shocked by her presence as well. Shocked, but grateful.

When at last she nodded, my heart stuttered then raced twice its normal pace. "Yes. I know Kiel."

Rezz's laughter broke the silence as those gathered roared their approval. But Rezz's roar of amusement was like thunder and he walked to me, slapped me on the back, hard. "Good luck with this one. I relinquish her protection to you."

Just like that, he was gone, sitting next to Braun in the stands. I looked at Warlord Braun, held his gaze, a question in my expression. Did he intend to challenge now that Rezz was out of the way?

Braun grinned at me and shook his head. No. I'd never fought in the pits, but Braun had seen me fight, really fight, when we took down a Hive Scout team a few days ago deep in a cavern. He was one of the few here who had seen me let the Hunter DNA loose in battle. I was fast, silent. Deadly.

Hunters of Everis were known across the entire galaxy as killers, hunters, assassins. We were assigned the most dangerous missions by the elite of the Coalition planets. We were feared and respected for being both merciless and deadly. That was why Governor Maxim called me in to find the intruder and track the Hive spies hiding deep in the caves on the Colony. Our unique gifts gave Hunters the ability to track anyone or anything anywhere in the universe. It was an instinctive pull, the call of prey, and no amount of time nor distance would dull it once a Hunter set his sights on a target.

There was nowhere to run, nowhere to hide. And right now, the only person I cared about in the universe was sitting on the edge of this fighting pit. And two Prillon warriors were determined to take her from me. Even though I said she was my marked mate, they would not stand down.

Fools.

Captain Voth stepped closer. "We challenge you, Hunter. The female belongs to us."

I heard Rezzer roar with laughter yet again. That beast and I were going to have to have a conversation later about his sense of humor. Still, I couldn't stop the answering grin that lifted the corners of my mouth as I crouched to attack.

* * *

Lindsey

OH. My. God.

He was here. Not just here, but right in front of me. So close I could feel his heat. Smell him. He'd been closer in the dream, but that hadn't been real. I frowned. Had it? I'd dreamed of someone I'd never met, saw him in detail. No, I'd fucked him in detail and now he was standing before me. Bigger, hotter and better than ever.

Next to the huge aliens Rezzer and Braun, he was moderately sized. But even then, on Earth he would've been considered big as a linebacker, at least six-six. His hair shone, a soft blue-black that I longed to run my fingers through. The color was more vibrant, more real than in the dream. His skin was fair and looked human, not golden like the two sharp-featured aliens standing across from him in challenge. He wore a uniform not unlike mine, the armor looked a helluva lot better on him, hugging the defined muscles of his shoulders and tapered down to six-pack abs that made my mouth water. But it was his eyes that made my heart stutter, dark and almost...desperate. I couldn't deny him, not with those eyes, those lonely eyes.

When my gaze roved back up, I saw his hands. Big hands.

Not dinner plates, but strong. Blunt fingers that I knew could touch my body and bring me intense pleasure. I knew what they felt like on my breasts, brushing over my nipples. And lower down, I knew what they felt like deep inside, curling over my G-spot.

I hadn't seen it in the dream, but I couldn't miss it now. He had a mark on his palm. It was in the same place as mine. From here, the shape appeared to be identical. His mark was a little darker, but his skin was ruddier, as if he'd been outside in the sun.

As if my body knew what I was looking at, the mark on my palm chose that moment to flare to life and pulse, sending shockwaves of need straight to my core. I held onto the edge of the pit for dear life as my body tensed in response and my breasts grew heavy. Suddenly, everyone around us faded and all I could think about was hopping down off this wall, going up to him and throwing myself in his arms, demand that he take off his clothes and shove me against the wall of this arena...make me his. Forever.

That thought stopped me cold.

No. Not forever. This could not be forever. I had a little boy to get home to and Earth expressly forbid underage citizens from travelling off world. It was part of the coalition agreements and widely advertised. No woman with children could join the Interstellar Brides program or volunteer to serve as a warrior in the Coalition Fleet. It was forbidden.

Wyatt.

I took a deep breath and blinked away the fog of desire looking at Kiel caused. His chest heaved and he rubbed his palm on his thigh as if the mark on his hand had flared as well.

Was that what he meant when he told the big fighter we were *'marked mates'*? Was it because we shared a birthmark? *The mark?*

While I definitely wanted him to get me naked and fuck me again—for real this time—I didn't want to belong to him. I didn't want to be his marked mate. I didn't belong to anyone, couldn't belong to any man. Only Wyatt. I lived and fought and breathed for my son. Nothing could change that.

I'd completely forgotten that golden warriors had spoken a challenge until Kiel answered them.

"I accept," he said, his deep voice new and yet familiar all at once. His eyes remained on me, but I knew he spoke to the two aliens behind him. "But she belongs to me."

I gulped at that, squirmed too, at the finality of his tone, the searing look in his gaze.

"Then prepare yourself." The two lookalike aliens behind him eyed me as well. I had to guess they were some kind of pair, perhaps cousins, for their golden coloring was identical and so were their features. Only the silver Hive additions were different. One had his left arm mostly replaced by the smooth robot-looking elements. The other had that silver eye and a silver hand.

He moved to stand directly beside me where my legs hung over the edge of the fighting pit, then turned to face his opponents. I could feel the press of his shoulder against my thigh. "I will not leave my mate unprotected as I fight."

"She will be guarded." I glanced over my shoulder, saw that the giant called Rezz spoke. He'd moved seats, positioning himself directly behind me.

Mr. Dinner Plate, Braun, was right beside him. The big man nodded. "Yes. This challenge is sacred. She will be well guarded as you and the Prillons decide the outcome of your claims."

They were like an organized bunch of Neanderthals. There was honor among them, although they were going to fight—I hoped not to the death—for me. Did this mean that if Kiel didn't win, the cyborg twins would be dragging me off by the hair to their cave? And both of them wanted me? Did that mean that they would take me together?

I glanced at Kiel, saw the determination in his gaze. He was not worried about fighting two partially mutated aliens. No, he was very confident as he took out his weapon and dropped it on the ground next to him. Next he unbuckled the holster from his thigh. Oh yeah, that was hot.

But I almost fainted when he reached behind his head and tugged off his armored shirt exposing his bare back inch by delicious inch.

I whimpered. I did. I couldn't help it. My ovaries practically jumped for joy at seeing his bare torso. I'd thought the other aliens' shoulders were broad, but Kiel? He won the hot man contest.

Broad, well-muscled shoulders weren't just wide, they tapered dramatically into a narrow waist. I could practically see the muscles ripple and flex as he moved. Then he turned. "Oh my."

He looked to me at the exclamation and he grinned. Dammit. I couldn't compete against his hotness. While I liked him all alpha male protector, this wicked smile was like a drug to my hyped up senses. There was a distinct promise in that smile, one that made me think things I hadn't worried about in years, if ever.

Sex. Hot, sweaty, never-wanna-stop sex.

"Wait for me," he said, then turned to his competition.

Wait for me. Those words meant so many things. Wait for the fight to end? Wait for him to win me from all these other alien Neanderthals? Wait to jump his rock hard body? Wait for his hard cock to fill me up and make me whimper, scream, beg for more.

All of the above?

I glanced over my shoulder once again at the two giants who were to keep me safe. No, I wasn't going anywhere. The way the others had been fighting, perhaps even getting ready to brawl over me, I had no intention of moving. Kiel, I knew. Or at least I knew him from my dreams. I knew he wouldn't hurt me. I was safe with him. The others? Even after being among them for a few minutes, I sensed their honor. It was what drove them, what defined their rules. I doubted any of them would actually hurt me, but I didn't wish to be permanently claimed by some random alien. Not only would it sidetrack my snooping and reporting, but it might keep me from getting back to the shuttle. I had to be on that shuttle. There was no other choice, no matter how hot the alien who thought to claim me.

I needed to be back on board for the return trip to Earth in three days. No, less than that now. The seventy-two hour clock was ticking.

The three men moved, hands up, in a circle. The challengers had stripped to the waist and dropped their weapons as well. It appeared this would be decided with hand-to-hand combat.

I should have been nervous that Kiel would lose, but something in the way he moved was almost magical. The other aliens had massive chests and arms, their bodies large and built for war, but I barely glanced at them. I couldn't tear my eyes off Kiel.

When he moved, I swayed with him, as if I could feel his thoughts, his intention. The reaction was strange, but I felt linked to him somehow. One with him. And his confidence was obvious. There was no doubt in him. No fear.

His confidence calmed me as nothing else could have. He was not going to lose. He was…invincible.

Which didn't make any sense. The others were bigger. Stronger.

I bit my lip and glanced back at Rezz to gauge his reaction as the three in the pit circled one another. He caught me looking and lifted his chin toward the fight. "Your mate is a Hunter, little human. Watch, so you will understand what that truly means." He grunted and crossed his arms, leaning back with a chuckle. "As these fools are learning the hard way."

I turned back to the center and watched as the golden ones began to move away from each other to attack Kiel from two sides at once.

Their knees were bent and they looked like boxers from home, without the gloves. Based on the earlier fights I'd watched, this wasn't going to be pretty. I wasn't one for violence. Since I had Wyatt, I cringed when I saw overtly aggressive behavior. In general, I avoided conflict and I hated when someone got hurt. I disliked seeing the weak being taken advantage of. Penalized. Hurt. I'd loved Sunday football before Wyatt. I'd loved a good, hard-hitting hockey game. But becoming a mother had changed me in unexpected ways, not one of which I would trade for anything.

Just because someone was physically weak didn't mean they weren't strong. Wyatt was the strongest person I knew and yet he couldn't play on the neighborhood playground. Couldn't defend himself from older kids who commented on him being different since his injury. Weaker. Less.

One of the golden warriors punched out, missing Kiel by a foot or more. Kiel only grinned wider at his opponents feint. "You're wasting my time," he said.

Then he moved.

Moved wasn't quite the right word for it. He was a blur, his speed so great my eyes and mind couldn't keep up. I heard the sound of his fist landing on bone. A groan, a thud, a crack. One opponent fell to the ground in regular speed, his body landing with a hard thump. Dust kicked up around him. His friend remained standing a second longer before he, too, was on the ground bleeding from a hit to his face I hadn't seen fall.

Kiel stilled then. A sheen of sweat coated his body, his knuckles red, but otherwise he was unchanged.

The others? One was unconscious, the other had his forearm bent in a ninety-degree angle that caused bile to rise to my throat. Kiel stood over them for a moment, looking at the duo he'd just decimated, then turned to me.

His dark gaze met mine. Held. He walked toward me as I saw others move quickly to attend the injured fighters. They pulled out the blue-glowing wands again, waved them over their injured bodies.

I couldn't pay attention to the intriguing space-tool because Kiel took over my whole field of vision. He stepped close, closer still so that I had to part my knees so he could settle between them. I felt his hips on the inside of my thighs, saw the black shadow of stubble on his jaw. The flecks of gold in his eyes.

"You are from Earth."

I nodded.

"Lindsey from Earth, you are my marked mate." He took my hand in his, lifted it so our fingers interlaced, our palms touched. Our *marks* touched.

I gasped at the searing heat of the contact, then nothing. No, not nothing. While the mark ceased to hurt entirely, I felt the connection elsewhere in my body. My breasts became heavy and achy, my nipples hardening into tight points. My pussy throbbed and I shifted my hips toward him so I could touch him with more than just my hand. I wanted to rub my clit against his cock, even through his pants, and come. I knew what it would feel like from the dream and I craved it.

I saw the same heat flare in his eyes, knew he felt it too. He leaned into me, gave me what I needed. I felt the hard press of his body against mine. My breasts pressed into his hard chest. His cock—god, yes!—pressed into me and I felt every thick, long inch of him against my lower belly.

"The dream," I murmured.

"Besides the mark—" He squeezed my hand where we touched. "—the dream proves you are mine. And I am yours."

He grinned and I saw a dimple. My panties were ruined now.

He leaned close so his warm breath fanned my ear, so only I could hear. "I want to feel your pussy clenching down on me again, feel you drip all over my cock. Taste you on my tongue. Breathe in the scent of your arousal."

He took a deep breath in through his nose. "Mmm. I can smell your pussy, mate."

Oh my god. I was going to come from just his dirty talk.

"Hunter Kiel. Take your mate and go." I didn't move. Neither did Kiel at the words. The order came from behind me, so it was either the Rezz or Mr. Dinner Plate. "You have defeated Voth and his second. No one else stands in challenge."

One second I was looking into Kiel's dark eyes, the next his grip released, moved to my waist and tossed me over his shoulder. My hands landed on his ass as he started to walk away. His very firm, very tight ass.

"Hunter, what of the intruder?" someone said.

I couldn't believe he was having a conversation as I was slung about like a sack of grain.

"The intruder has been found and detained. Please inform the governor that I will see to her. Personally."

When his hand settled on the back of my upper thigh, his fingers slipping inward and brushing over my pussy, I knew just how he was going to *see to me.*

"Hurry," I whispered, wanting the dream all over again, but this time, for real. Maybe I couldn't keep him, but I could have him for now. And with the shitstorm my life had been the last few years, I wasn't above chasing a few hours of heaven on this strange, alien world.

His pace increased as a growl rumbled through him and into me.

* * *

"THERE ARE MANY QUESTIONS BETWEEN US," Kiel said after he lowered me back to my feet. He hadn't stopped walking for a few minutes. I heard other footsteps, saw the legs and feet of two warriors who followed, but none spoke. From being upside-down, I could only tell that the ground continued to be rocky and the interior of the building he took me into had sleek black floors.

"Yes." With one hand on my arm, he ensured I gained my balance. We appeared to be in his living quarters. No one else was about. The space was modern, sparse and neat. It was a cross between a stateroom on a cruise ship—I'd gone once when I was a teenager with a girlfriend whose family had enough money to take me with them—and a military barrack. There was a window, although it was tinted like a car window and I could barely see out. A desk and a chair, a bed and another door, which I had to guess led to an en suite bathing room.

But Kiel wasn't talking about questions of his living space. No. He was talking about everything else. The mark. The heat. The dream. The fight. My presence on the base. The magic blue wands. The attraction between us. The need to fuck him that was clawing away at my insides like acid, making me burn and hurt. I needed to touch him so badly my body actually ached.

Everything.

I could ask him questions all day long. The same could be

said for him. His mate was being fought over in an arena full of aliens. No, they weren't aliens to him. In an arena full of warriors. He hadn't been pleased. He'd been possessive. He still was. I felt it, along with the growing attraction, coming from him.

"I don't understand this thing between us," I replied. "The dream? How were you in my dream?"

He leaned in, lifted a gentle hand to grace my cheek. That simple touch melted me and I was ready to give him anything he wanted.

This wasn't like me. I'd never really been hot and bothered for any man my entire life. Even the sperm donor never managed to really get me hot.

But this? Kiel was burning me alive.

"Do you want me? Do you feel the fire burning between us?"

I nodded, trapped in his gaze. I couldn't deny it.

"Then let's both ask our questions later." His eyes met mine as if looking for a tacit agreement. Consent. "I want to touch you."

Later, as in, *Fuck now, talk later.*

I doubted a professional spy shared her dreams with an alien, got discovered within minutes of arriving on a new planet, fought over by a horde of Hive contaminated warriors and then claimed by a marked mate. I doubted a real spy would want to fuck the man who'd fought and won her in some kind of archaic, chest-pounding testosterone fest.

Well, I wasn't a spy. But I was starting to think the marked mate thing might have some truth. Same with his one word. *Later.*

"Later," I agreed. *Fuck now, talk later.*

Since he hadn't put on his shirt since the fight, it made things easy. I closed the slight distance between us and put my hands on his solid torso. Oh yeah. Hot skin, soft and smooth. Beneath, hard pecs, ridged abs. I worked his belt open with a need I had never known before. I wanted him naked. Now.

I wasn't a virgin. I had Wyatt and it hadn't been immaculate conception. But his father had truly been a mistake, a guy who ran the moment things got serious. I considered him nothing more than a sperm donor. At the time, it had been a stupid mistake.

When Wyatt was born, I'd had no interest in sex. Between pushing out a watermelon and nursing him, my body was a no-go zone. By the time my libido returned, I was working two jobs and going to school. I never had time for sleep, let alone a lukewarm hour in bed with a man I didn't love. I barely had time to shower and shave my legs, let alone have a relationship.

To say the dream I'd shared with Kiel had been the hottest sex I'd ever had wasn't an exaggeration. I'd actually come and not by my fingers. I wanted that again. Now.

I was leaving in seventy hours. I could go for it. It was like the old saying, *What happens in space, stays in space.*

His pants parted and I curled my fingers around the top and tugged, working his pants down, but the material was caught. On his cock. Carefully, I worked his clothing past the thick bulge and when his long, hard cock was free of the confines, it bounced out. Yes, bounced. It was stiff and long and pointed upward, directly at me.

"Wow."

Yeah, it wasn't the most intelligent thing to say, but when there was an incredible cock *right there* and it was hard just for me. My mind went blank. I took in the ruddy color of it, a few shades darker than the rest of him. There was a pulsing vein that ran up the length of it, showing off the inches and inches of thick dick. God, my thoughts sounded like a porn flick, but this cock?

Wow.

The head was broad, like a fireman's hat. The flared ridge made me clench my inner walls, knowing it would slide and rub over every needy nerve ending in my pussy.

Kiel's hands were at his sides, but I saw his fingers curl into fists as if he was holding back from touching me. I saw a drop of pre-cum ooze from the narrow slit at the tip and I licked my lips. I flicked a glance up at Kiel, saw the heat and anticipation in his eyes. He was waiting to see what I'd do.

He was the one exposed. I was still fully dressed, allowing me to make a choice about what happened. Yes, he wanted to fuck me. And he probably would even if he had to coax me slowly into it. But that wasn't going to be necessary.

Hell, no.

I looked to his cock again and then dropped to my knees, the pulsing flesh inches from my face. His growl of need was replaced by a roar of pleasure when my tongue flicked out and I licked up that drop of fluid.

I'd read some romance novels, some pretty kinky ones at that, and I'd been wet and hot afterwards. I'd pulled out my vibrator and made myself come, fantasizing about the hero.

I'd thought that was arousal. No, that hadn't been anything. Tepid interest at best. This, with Kiel? It was like an inferno. The longer I was with him, the more eager I became. Needy. Desperate. Frantic for him.

I wouldn't be on my knees learning his taste otherwise. I didn't jump to a blow job. That wasn't me. I liked to kiss a man on his mouth before I would even consider giving a good blow job. But with Kiel? All rules were gone. There was no playbook for this. I was driven by desire. And I wanted him to tremble at my touch. I wanted to conquer him. I wanted him so mad with lust, so desperate for me that he threw me down on that bed and fucked me until I begged for mercy.

With my right hand, I gripped the base of his cock, my fingers not closing around it completely. Would that fit in me? Could I take something so broad? So long? So damn hard?

I'd worry about that later. Now I wanted to feel him on my tongue, to have more of his flavor—salty and almost tart. More fluid came and I collected it all as his hand rested gently on top of my head. When I began to lick the crown like an ice cream cone, his fingers curled, tightened.

When I parted my lips, opened wide and took him into my mouth, he tugged on my hair. He groaned and my own sounds of pleasure caused by the slightly painful pull on my hair was lost.

My free hand went to his thigh for balance, my palm on his uniform pants and my fingers resting on his bare skin, the springy hair there awakening my senses further.

I couldn't take all of him. I wasn't a porn star, although I doubted they'd be able to do it either. He was just too... much. And so I worked him as I could moving so I took him as deep as I could into my mouth, then back, my fist sliding and twisting up and down to hopefully soothe all of him.

"Lindsey." The word was a bark, rough and guttural and it made goosebumps rise on my skin.

His fingers tugged, pulling me off of him completely. I looked up at him through my lashes. "You want me to stop?"

Eyes widening, he almost looked mad. "Gods, no. But I'm going to come within seconds like an untried youth. While I'd love to fuck your sweet mouth, I am far from done and I want to come deep in your pussy."

This was how women became pregnant. Thank god for the Depo shot my ob-gyn gave me last month. No babies for me. The shot would prevent a pregnancy, which meant I could just enjoy the moment. I loved my son, but he was all I could handle right now, alone and struggling to take care of him.

But Kiel? This heat? This was for me. For the first time in years, I was going to take something for myself.

And I wanted this gorgeous hunk of a warrior.

No regrets. No mistakes. Being with Kiel was too powerful, too perfect for regrets. There was no doubt to his virility. His balls were large and hung heavily between his strong thighs. I was prepared to lay back and let him fuck me right now, just from the taste of him on my tongue, the carnal words he uttered.

I wasn't thinking about anything but having him inside me, stretching me open, filling me up. I was reckless, wild. Uninhibited.

I had Wyatt to go home to, but this? This was just a wild night that I so, so needed. No strings. No repercussions. Nothing but a hot alien fling. Tomorrow I'd learn more about this world, especially that blue wand thing that seemed to heal. If it healed big fighters with broken bones, then surely it could heal Wyatt's leg. I was on the right track here. Get info, get the story, get money and get a space wand to heal my child. I might have been discovered, but things were working out. Especially since I had a mostly naked hot alien ready to fuck me like a caveman.

My mind was eased and so when he took hold of my wrist and tugged me to my feet, I didn't think. I went willingly, surrendering control. I'd already made the decision to give myself to him. Now, all I wanted to do was hold on for the ride.

iel

I KNEW THIS WAS COMPLICATED. There was much to learn from Lindsey, the Earth woman who'd appeared from nowhere on the planet. Maxim would want to talk with her. How had she come to be in the air ducts? Why was she here? How had she gotten into the main area cargo hold? Krael had destroyed the peaceful balance on the planet, the illusion of safety and everyone was nervous. Fearful. Warriors had died and many worried they might be next. While we were in exile, we were also supposed to be safe. Female mates now worked and lived among us.

I didn't give a shit about any of it. I only cared about Lindsey. I should have handed her over to Maxim. I should have asked her all the questions that were piling up in my mind. But she was my marked mate and that trumped everything.

I didn't need answers from her to know she wasn't a traitor. I didn't care what miracle had brought her to me or why she'd magically appeared. It didn't matter. She was mine. And she'd just sucked my cock with an eagerness that had my balls drawing up and my orgasm building at the base of my spine. I wanted nothing more than to come in the tight, wet heat of her mouth, but I wanted her pussy instead. I wanted to sink deep, become one with her and fill her up. Knowing the power of the marks, my need for her would only get more intense.

I sensed her need as well, knew it would only become more and more severe until I ultimately did claim her. I ached to bond her to me, but there were too many things unspoken between us. When I made her mine forever, she needed to know what was happening and make the choice. Choose me.

Until then, we'd learn each other's bodies. I would discover what made her hot, what made her moan. I'd make her come over and over until only my name filled her thoughts, only the pleasure I could give her blinded her from everything that stood between us. There was much, but it would wait.

Fucking her would not.

Once I had her on her feet again, I placed my hands on her small shoulders and started to walk her backwards toward the bed. "You're wearing too many clothes," I told her.

"I am."

I didn't need to ask her consent; she'd been on her knees sucking me off. I'd stop if she wanted, but when she lifted her shirt armor over her head, I had my answer.

When her underclothes were revealed, I froze in place, mesmerized.

She toed off one boot, then the other before working her pants off her flared hips.

"What the hell is that?"

She looked down at her perfect body, at the red, sheer scraps that were intermixed with shiny fabric and covered her small breasts. Lower, a matching triangle covered her pussy. Thin, delicate straps rode over her hips and disappeared behind her. Hooking one hand on her hip, I spun her about, saw that there was absolutely no fabric covering her ass, just a thin red string that disappeared between the heart-shaped cheeks of her ass. I spun her back around so she faced me again.

Looking up at me, a coy smile played across her lips. "You like?"

"Like?" I repeated, my voice a snarl. I'd never seen anything like it before. It was alluring, enticing and teased me as to what was beneath. I couldn't see her nipples other than the hard outline of them through the flimsy garment, but I imagined their color.

I stepped back, gripped my cock and began to slowly stroke it, trying to ease the ache.

"That can't be legal on Earth."

She laughed then, running the backs of her fingers over the soft curve of one breast, then the other. "Should I take it off then?"

Slowly, I shook my head. "No. That's my job." I continued to stroke myself. "Lay back on the bed."

My mate was a vixen. She turned about, put one knee up on the soft mattress and crawled across it, her ass on perfect display, that little line of red taunting me with what was hidden. With my free hand, I reached out and gave one pert cheek a swat. Instantly, a handprint bloomed that matched her meager covering.

She squealed, then flipped onto her back, propped up on her elbows. There was no anger in her pale gaze, only heat. Banked heat. It was time to stoke it.

I let go of my cock. While it throbbed with need, it would have to wait. I had things to do to my mate first.

I gripped one slim ankle and slid it outward on the bed, parting her legs. From this angle, I could see the red fabric covering her pussy was dark, stained with her arousal. My mouth watered for a taste of her.

Grabbing her other ankle, I pulled her toward me, then I knelt on the floor right at the edge of the bed. Hooking the back of her knees now, I pulled her even closer to me, slipping one leg, then the other, over my shoulders. She was so small, so slight that I was afraid I was being too rough, but there was no complaint, only a breathy moan of surprise.

Her pussy was right before me. I took a deep breath. This... *this* was not in the dream we shared. Her ripe, dark scent made pre-cum slip from my cock in a steady stream. With the tip of one finger, I touched the delicate material.

"What are these called?"

She was still up on her elbows watching me. "My panties?"

I slid my fingertip over every inch of the *panties.*

"They are regulation clothing for Earth warriors?"

She shook her head. "I wasn't expecting anyone to see them."

I growled then, the idea of someone else seeing this sexy display. It only spurred me on, to learn everything about her, *see* every bit of her.

I knew I brushed over her clit when her legs tensed against my shoulders. Sliding along the edge, I hooked my finger in, slid the fabric to the side and I saw her for the first time.

Pink and slick, her flesh was bare. Swollen. Perfect.

I gave her one quick glance, saw the way she bit her lip as if keeping herself from begging, then I lowered my head.

Tasted her.

Her hand went to my head, tangled in my hair. Tugged. The slight bite of pain only enhanced my pleasure. I wasn't gentle. I couldn't be, yet I would never hurt her.

No, I pushed her ruthlessly to the brink, the taste of her coating my tongue, engrained in my mind, my senses.

She was so responsive, so wet I lapped it all up as I flicked her clit with my tongue.

"Please," she begged, her heels pressing into my back and pulling me closer.

I couldn't deny her. Not now. Another time, perhaps, when our lovemaking was playful. This first time was anything but.

Urgent.

Frantic.

Wild.

Abandoned.

Slipping two fingers into her, I curled them, immediately found the spongy spot that had her chin point up to the ceiling and her scream fill the air. I didn't stop with my tongue, pushing the pleasure through her as her pussy clutched and tugged at my fingers, pulling them into her as if she needed more.

She did. My mouth wasn't enough. It never would be.

I rose to my feet, wiped my mouth with the back of my hand, then stripped. I was quick about it, eager to feel her again. I enjoyed the way her eyes widened at the sight of me, flared with heat. *I* was enjoying the way she lay before me, legs spread, pussy peeking out from the dainty edge of her panties. Lifting one hand, she reached out. I batted it away, took hold of the thin line of red on her hips and tugged at the material, ripping it from her body. She was now naked before me except for the sexy-as-fuck covering on her breasts.

"How do you take that off?" I asked, pointing.

She kept her eyes on me as her hands somehow undid a front clasp between her breasts. The garment parted and her small, perfectly round globes appeared.

I growled.

"I will fuck you now. Yes?" I asked, my voice rough. I would resist my basest of needs if she said no, but when she nodded her head and breathed, "Yes," I hooked her knees again, aligned my cock and slid into her.

"Oh god," she said, her eyes falling closed.

"Fuck," I murmured. My feet were on the floor and I had perfect leverage to slide into her in one long, slick slide. I bottomed out and she clenched and squeezed me, her pussy walls adjusting to being so open for me.

With one hand behind a knee still, I leaned forward, planted a palm on the bed beside her head.

"Look at me," I said.

Her eyes fluttered open, the pale color now a dark and stormy green.

"I want to watch as you come, feel it when you pulse all over my cock."

Her walls clenched again. I pulled back, thrust deep.

"This pussy, it's mine."

She cried out.

Dropping my head, I took one nipple in my mouth and felt it harden against my tongue.

Her back arched and her hands slid up and down my back, her nails scoring me.

My orgasm built at the base of my spine, drew up my balls. I couldn't stop, couldn't do anything but pump into her, stroke her walls with my cock, to feel every slick inch of her.

"You will come again," I said.

It was bossy and very presumptuous, but she was my mate and I knew exactly what she needed. Knew she would come because I bid it, just as I could not hold back my own pleasure.

Her muscles tightened, her body stilling as she came, her inner walls milking me. She didn't scream this time; she had no voice, only her mouth wide open as she rode out the pleasure I gave her.

Her orgasm was mine. I gave it to her.

"Mine," I roared as *she* gave me what I'd craved forever. This wasn't just jerking off. This wasn't a quick tumble. No, this was my mate and we were everything.

My orgasm roared through me, my seed bursting from my cock deep inside her, filling her, coating her. Marking her. It was not a claiming, but that would come soon.

For now, I slumped upon her, satisfied in knowing that she was here in my arms, my cock deep inside her. I found her and there was no way I would let her go.

* * *

Lindsey

THE GOVERNOR of this base was an alien, and he was scary. He didn't look remotely human, not like my Kiel. And he was huge, at least seven feet tall with shoulders twice the size of any normal man I'd ever seen. His name was Maxim and his skin was a rich, dark copper color. His eyes were the color of coffee and his hair was nearly black. His features were pointed, his nose a bit too sharp, chin and cheekbones too angular to be human. And he was not very happy with me at the moment. Neither was his mate, Rachel.

They'd brought her in after the first hour. Maybe thinking I'd change my story.

I wouldn't. I couldn't. Yes, I was lying, but I had no choice.

If I didn't make it back to Earth, they'd hurt my son. Maybe kill him. I took a deep breath and tightened my grip on the edges of the too big chair I sat in. My feet swung below me like I was in kindergarten again. I felt small and vulnerable. And I hated that feeling.

"I told you. I'm a reporter. There's a huge paycheck out there for stories about the Colony."

"Try again, Lindsey. We're not buying what you're selling." That was his mate, Rachel, talking. Her arms were crossed, and I knew that look. She was from Earth, like me. Her accent was American, like me. But unlike me, she seemed happy to be here. She wore a dark green uniform, which I'd learned meant she worked in the medical station. On Earth, she'd been a biochemist or something like that. Something with way too much math and science for my tastes.

Unfortunately, she was brilliant, and I felt like a chastised schoolgirl. I worried she could see right through me. The way Kiel was looking at me wasn't helping. Of everyone here, lying to him was the hardest. I wanted to throw myself in his arms, have a two hour crying jag, and let him take care of everything. Unfortunately, he was exiled to the Colony and I had to get home, light years away. Wyatt needed me. And as wonderful and amazing as being with Kiel had been, it had also been bittersweet because I knew I couldn't stay. I was not that kind of mother. My son came first. And if that meant I had to live without Kiel, without anyone for me, well, Wyatt would have to be enough.

I closed my eyes, remembered his sweet dimples, trusting blue eyes, and that soft little hand in mine. Just thinking about him made my chest ache. His happiness was more important than mine. He was more important than I could ever be. What was I? A washed up college grad who couldn't keep a man interested once a kid was involved?

No. I was a mother. I was raising a young man to be better than his father. And that had to be enough. No, it would be enough. Steeling myself, I opened my eyes and looked Rachel straight in the eye as I lied.

"It's a hundred grand, Rachel." I shrugged and tried to look sheepish, innocent, clueless and as harmless as possible. "There will be more reporters coming."

"Seriously?" Rachel rolled her eyes. "That's crazy."

"Enquiring minds," I offered. "Since the death of Captain Brooks, there are conspiracy theorists burning up the internet with all kinds of crazy stories." Swinging my hands through the air to indicate the entire base, or even planet, I continued, "They think this is some kind of prison. That the Coalition is taking our soldiers and locking them up here without due process. That they are being tortured and denied their freedom, little better than slaves. And there are a lot of people who believe it."

She rolled her eyes. "Jeez. No wonder they've had trouble recruiting from Earth the last few months." Rachel muttered.

"The number of warriors from Earth has fallen since Brooks's death. My brother told me the number of new warriors has decreased by half." Maxim's dark brows drew together in an alien version of a scowl and I leaned away instinctively, but Kiel was there. When his hand came to rest on my shoulder, I could think again. He wasn't mine, but he wouldn't let anything happen to me. I knew that with a certainty that made my entire body hurt at the thought of leaving him behind. But he was Colony. An alien. And I had to go home.

I hadn't really considered the wider implications of all this. Or what would happen if Earth didn't send the promised number of fighters for the war. That wasn't my problem, or I hadn't thought it had been. Until now. How had those issues affected this interrogation? "What will happen to Earth if we don't send enough soldiers?"

"Or brides," Rachel added.

"We will take what we need," Maxim replied without hesitation. "Earth cannot be allowed to fall." He paced for a moment before walking to a control screen as I looked to Kiel for an explanation.

"How many people live on Earth, Lindsey?"

I shook my head. "I don't know. Eight or nine billion. Something like that."

I saw Rachel nod out of the corner of my eye.

"And they'd all be turned into Hive," Rachel added. "Better to save them now than fight them later, after they've been integrated."

Integrated. The word sent an ice-cold shiver up my spine.

My gaze followed Maxim as he brought up an image on the wall screen in front of him. I tensed, recognizing the stark white and gray walls, the polished floor, the Interstellar Brides Program insignia on the uniform of the woman who turned to face the screen. I hadn't ever spoken to her, but I'd seen her when the others sneaked me inside the building to be hidden inside the cargo ship.

"Warden Egara. Greetings from the Colony." Maxim bowed slightly and the Earth woman smiled. Her hair was dark brown and pulled back into a bun, like a ballerina might wear. The look made her appear to be much more severe and serious than her age would suggest. She was quite pretty, and not much older than me.

"Maxim. Rachel! How are you?"

Rachel was smiling and it was obvious the two women were friends, or at least liked each other. "I'm wonderful. Thank you."

The warden nodded and turned her full attention to the governor, narrowing her eyes. "Not that I don't enjoy hearing from you, Maxim, but it's usually not good news. What can I do for you?"

"You are correct. Not good news." Maxim turned to me and motioned with his hand for me to step forward. Reluctantly, I did. I had no choice. "This woman managed to make her way to the Colony on one of the large transport cruisers from Earth. I need to know who helped her and why."

The warden's eyes widened, then fell and that no-nonsense gaze turned to me. "Who are you, dear?"

I cleared my throat. "My name is Lindsey Walters. I'm a reporter."

I heard her quick inhale. "A reporter? For who?"

"Freelance."

"I see." She tilted her head, staring at me, but talking to Maxim. "Does she have an NPU?"

Maxim reached for me, but Kiel stepped between us before Maxim's hands made contact with the side of my face. "Don't touch her."

Warden Egara's eyes widened. "Lift your hand, Lindsey. I need to see your palm."

Oh, shit. I knew exactly what she wanted, so I raised my other hand, the one without the mark.

No fooling her. "The other one, too."

Crap. I lifted my other hand, palm toward the screen and she leaned back as if shocked.

"You carry the mark of Everis."

Okay. That was a new one. But I knew it was what made the chemistry between me and Kiel so insta-hot. Lowering my hand, I waited to see what would happen next. But the warden was efficient, and single-minded. She looked to Kiel.

"Hunter, does she have an NPU?"

Kiel lifted his gaze to her. "You know what I am?"

"Of course. I have sent a dozen marked mates to the Cornerstone in Everis. I've seen the mark before."

Kiel nodded, accepting her explanation as my mind whirled with questions. Marked mates? The cornerstone? Everis? Was that Kiel's planet before…?

"Does she have an NPU?" the warden asked again.

Kiel's hand lifted to trace the odd bump under my skin where that ice-cold doctor had inserted a needle that looked at least three times bigger than it needed to be. "Yes. She does. But unless she is a Coalition linguistics expert, that was already obvious."

The warden asked us all to wait for a minute and we watched her walk over to a set of smaller screens, like a computer workstation. When she returned, her gaze was nowhere close to friendly. "The only transport sent to the Colony left from the Miami processing station." I would have sworn she snarled at me. "My station."

Yes. She was right. I'd been in that building, sneaked right past her. I couldn't hold her gaze. I wasn't a great liar anyway. About this, I wasn't even going to try.

"Who helped you?" she asked. "Who gave you the NPU? Who got you on board that ship?"

Kiel spoke to her, but he was looking at me, his hand wrapped around the back of my neck in a blatant display of ownership I didn't have the heart to reject at the moment. He was the only pseudo-friendly person in the room. The feel of his hand was reassuring, and very possessive. "She also arrived with full battle armor with life support capabilities."

The warden whistled. "You've got rich friends."

I shook my head. "They're not my friends. They just really want this story."

"What story?" Warden Egara asked.

Well, this was one part of the truth I could tell them. "They think this place is a prison and that our troops are being sent up here to be some kind of alien slaves. They sent me here to sneak around, take video and write an exposé on this prison planet and the horrible war crimes our troops are suffering."

The governor cleared his throat. "That's ridiculous. It's Earth who refuses to accept her own warriors once they've been contaminated. They are here because they are denied permission to return home."

"What?" I spun around to look at him. "What the hell are you talking about?"

Rachel rubbed her temples with both hands. "Good God. What a joke." She looked up at the warden. "We'll find out who sent her here and get the information back to you."

"Thank you. I'll be waiting." The warden nodded once more, scowled at me like I'd just killed her puppy, and the screen want blank.

But Rachel wasn't done with me. She spun on her heel, her eyes flashing. "You've got some nerve."

"Who betrayed us on Earth? Who sent you here?" Maxim demanded.

"I'm a reporter. I'm sorry. I can't reveal my sources." It was weak. Lame. If they wanted to torture me, beat the truth out of me, they could try. All I cared about now was getting back to Wyatt. I had enough of a story from what they were saying to know that the Colony had a public relations problem on Earth more than anything sinister going on here. At least, if I believed what was being said around me. Which I did.

"All right. If you want to share the truth about the Colony, then we will give you the truth. Not the blatant lies being spread on Earth." Maxim looked down on me with a new expression on his face. I didn't know these aliens, and I couldn't read his expression well enough to know what he was thinking, but he didn't seem angry, so that was a bonus. "Kiel, give her recording equipment and take her on a tour of the base. Find the warriors from Earth and allow her to speak to them, learn their stories. Take your video footage. Look around, female. See the truth. Then we will send you home."

"What?" Rachel screeched as Kiel protested.

"No. She will stay."

I was already shaking my head slowly, over and over. No. No. No. I couldn't stay. I held Maxim's dark gaze, as he seemed to be the only sane person in the room at the moment. "I can't stay."

Rachel crossed her arms over her chest. "You can't let her go home, Maxim. God only knows what kind of lies she'll feed the press. We'll never get any mates to come here if she has her way."

"I wouldn't do that."

My protest was lost on deaf ears as Kiel's angry voice filled the room. "She must remain on the Colony."

Maxim's eyes narrowed as he considered Kiel's words, but I was still moving my head from side to side, unrelenting. "I have to go back to Earth. I'm not staying." I glanced back and saw raw fury and open pain in Kiel's eyes. The sight nearly broke me, but I had Wyatt. No matter how amazing, wonderful and sexy Kiel was, no matter how smoking hot his kiss, no matter the mind-shattering orgasms he gave me...I had to get back to my son. "I can't stay here."

Maxim spoke. "She is not part of the Interstellar Brides Program. She does not belong to the Coalition. She is not contaminated. If she does not wish to remain, we must send her home. Coalition protocol demands her safe return to her home planet." Maxim's words were like a death knell in the room and he cleared his throat, clearly unhappy. "Via transport this time. Am I understood?"

Rachel lifted her hand to her neck as if something pained her and her skin paled, as if she were about to faint.

But Maxim was talking to me, so I nodded, relieved that I

wasn't going to be kept a prisoner on this strange planet. "Yes, sir. Thank you."

"We will give you the access you traveled so far for. So you may see the truth. Hear it. You will return to the Miami transport station, where I am quite sure Warden Egara will want to have a word with you."

"Okay." Whatever. I wasn't a prisoner here. I wouldn't be a prisoner once I got home, either. The warden wouldn't be able to stop me from getting to my son.

It was my turn to clear my throat, fighting back tears at the idea of leaving Kiel behind. "When can I go home?"

Maxim studied me another moment as I ignored everyone and everything else in the room. "How much time do you need to gather information for your report?"

I had no idea, but not long. "A day. Maybe two."

"One day. You leave this time tomorrow. If you aren't going to stay, I want you gone as quickly as possible." His gaze darted to Kiel, who was pacing behind me.

"One day," I repeated. That should be more than long enough. By tomorrow afternoon, I'd be back in the main command building, in the transport room, on my way home to Wyatt.

And I was going to make sure I had one of those blue healing things when I went.

My hand was a fist at my side as I buried my pain at leaving Kiel. He was so angry at the possibility. No, not possibility. Reality. Fuck the people who sent me here. Fuck Wyatt's doctors and their high dollar surgeries. I'd seen that blue wand heal worse than the broken growth plates in Wyatt's leg bones. Surely one of those wands would be able to heal him, make him run and play again. Give him back his laughter. Coming this far, knowing that technology exists and leave it behind? Not happening. I'd find one and sneak it out.

Wyatt would be healed, but I'd be broken. At least my heart. One day was all I had left with Kiel.

As if he read my mind, he moved into place behind me, his hands on my shoulders. I felt the possession of his weighted touch, the heat of it. "No. She is my marked mate, Maxim. We must petition Prime Nial for an exception."

Maxim's entire demeanor changed and his gaze snapped to Kiel's, his attention over my head. "Are you certain? There is no room for a mistake. Not in this."

"She's mine." Kiel's voice had dropped to a soft, threatening tone that made my heart race and my pussy wet. "I'm very sure. We've been dream sharing since her arrival."

Dream sharing. So, I wasn't going crazy? That dream I'd had when I was sleeping in that freight container had been *real*? It was a thing?

"She's mine," he repeated and the governor nodded in acceptance.

God, yes, I was his, but it didn't matter. I couldn't stay. "I have to go home," I repeated. Nothing had changed. Not one damn thing.

"I will contact Prime Nial at once." The governor ignored me and spoke to Kiel as if my choice no longer mattered. Fine, I was his marked mate, but that didn't mean I would choose him over Wyatt.

"Thank you, Maxim."

"What? No! This is bullshit, Maxim—" Rachel's protest faded as my head spun.

What the hell had just happened? One moment I was all set with a guided tour and a quick transport home. And now? "Who is Prime Nial?" I asked.

Kiel's hand slid to the small of my back, pushing me out of the door even as I heard Rachel continue her protests. Seemed she was not as inclined to be nice to me as her mate. For some reason, she was like a mother bear and protective of her cubs—alien cubs at that—when someone came after them. She was trying to protect these big, burly men from the likes of me. If it wasn't so necessary, it would be funny.

While she was in protective mode, the governor was pouring on the politics. He had to get Earth to play nice with the Colony, to make this place seem...positive. He was hoping I'd meet the warriors, interview them, and write something that would make the Colony look good, make the Coalition Fleet look good.

Public relations were a bitch when they were trying to sell a war, especially to an entire planet of people light years away.

At least, that's how things had been going...until Kiel turned caveman. "Who is Prime Nial?" I asked again with a sharper tone.

Kiel stopped me in the corridor outside the meeting room and pushed my back to the wall. Before I could protest, his mouth was on mine. Hot. Hard. Demanding.

I had no hope of resisting and I opened for him, welcomed the sweep of his tongue in my mouth as he groaned, his hands dropping to my hips as he pressed his hard length to mine. My mind drifted to naked places when he tore his lips from mine and buried his nose in my hair, drawing my scent into his lungs. "Prime Nial is the ruler of Prillon Prime, the leader of the Prillon people, and commander of the entire Coalition Fleet."

Holy shit. And they were calling this guy? About me? "Why are you contacting him? Why would he care about me? I'm just a woman from Earth."

Kiel nuzzled my neck, just below my ear, and I melted into him. God, he was so damn irresistible. The mark on my hand was on fire, so hot I rubbed the wicked flesh over my thigh to try to get it to stop burning. "Because you're mine. Rachel is here from Earth because she was matched through the Interstellar Brides program. Kristin, too. Yet you came through...less legal channels. It matters not to me, only that you are here and that you are mine now."

I sighed, and I knew the sound was pitiful and sad. "I can't stay, Kiel."

He growled softly, his hands wrapping beneath me to cup my ass. "You can, mate. You're mine and I'm not letting you go. The Prime will petition Earth for an exception."

"An exception?"

His lips were hot against my neck. "He makes the rules. He can change them. No one can doubt we are matched mates. That stands above any laws, any rules from any planet."

Oh, shit. He was saying because I had the mark on my hand, because we dream shared, because I wanted him with an obsession that made my heart pound, that rules would be bent and broken so I could remain with him. I couldn't let this happen. I had to go home. "I'm not your mate."

"You are." He lifted me, my back sliding along the wall as he positioned my clit over the hard, thick bulge of his cock through his uniform. My gasp of surprise turned into a moan of need as my pussy flooded with wet heat and my breasts grew heavy. I dropped my forehead to his shoulder, clung to him with a desperation I did not recognize in myself. Why? Why did I have to react to him like this? Why couldn't I have the hots for an Earth man? Surely there had to be one guy on that planet who would make me feel this way.

"What if I say no? I read that Interstellar Brides have thirty days to decide. Don't I get thirty days? Won't this prime guy say I have thirty days, too?"

"Yes, mate. Most likely." Kiel stilled, his back stiffening as he settled me on my feet and stepped away. His gaze was dark and brooding, hurt. But I couldn't let that affect me.

With Wyatt's future on the line, I didn't dare do anything

but exactly what I'd promised. I'd return to Earth with the truth. I'd give the people who hired me raw data, interviews and video. How they decided to spin it was up to them. If they wanted photos of frightening aliens on a prison planet, that's what I've give them.

No one was going to hurt my baby. No one.

"Shall we begin the tour?" I asked.

Kiel scowled at me, but silently led the way.

CHAPTER 6

MY MATE DECIDED that the best way to discover the truth was to do interviews with the warriors living on the Colony. To get information from those that lived here. It seemed reasonable, but I didn't care. I didn't care that a planet halfway across the galaxy learned the truth about us. I had no opinion, as the only thing I cared about was keeping her with me. It was my job as her mate to keep her safe and happy. Nothing more. Maxim and Prime Nial could deal with Earth.

Maxim had agreed to petition the Prime to allow an exception to be made for Lindsey. Thank the gods, because I could not give her up. Every instinct, every cell in my body was utterly and completely hers. Just the thought of being separated from her in less than a day made me angry.

"Let's set up the camera and mic over there." Lindsey pointed to the end of a dining hall table in the main meal room. While each person's quarters had a food unit, it was recommended—and observed—that everyone ate together. Since we all came from being held captive by the Hive, it was important for everyone to bond, to create a new bond, a new family of sorts.

The space was bright with light from the two suns shining through the wall of windows. It was a welcoming spot, intended to pull people together, to see their new world in all its rugged beauty through the glass.

I didn't have as difficult a time as some did, trying to assimilate. But then, I understood the promise, how family and community worked. Hunters from Everis weren't the best trackers because we didn't understand how people worked, how they thought and felt, what they wanted.

No, we were the best because we did understand, and used the very emotional need for connection or recognition to good use. Even now, a handful of warriors lingered in the large room, clearly off duty at the moment, playing a game of chance with cards and numbered stones. Two were Prillon warriors I recognized, Captains Marz and Trax. An Atlan sat opposite them, Warlord Rezzer, whom I would owe a life-long debt for protecting my mate in the fighting pits until I could arrive. Holding her own amongst the warriors, and the final player, was another human female. Kristin. She was small, but opposite my mate in every other way.

Lindsey had long golden hair, Kristin's was of a similar color, but short, shorter even than Rezzer's. Kristin was voluptuous with large breasts and full lips. Lindsey was lean, with small breasts, a muscular abdomen and a curved ass so perfect I couldn't keep my hands off her. Like Lindsey, Kristin was from Earth. Unlike Lindsey, she'd volunteered to be a bride and eagerly mated to Tyran and Hunt upon her arrival. She wasn't going home. *This* was her home now.

The group seated here, waiting for us, were my friends. My investigation team. The group I worked with on a daily basis to find Krael. My fellow Hunters, or as close as I was going to find on a planet where I was the only one of my kind.

I was the only one from Everis. The only one with a strange mark on my palm that had pulsed and come to life, that was pushing me to claim Lindsey and fighting with every atom of my being to keep her with me.

Isolation. Loneliness. I was no stranger to the darkness of true separation. I'd been so alone for a very long time. From the time I joined the Elite Hunters unit, to my confinement and torture with the Hive. And finally, here. The Colony. A prison without bars. A lifelong death sentence, especially if Lindsey returned to Earth.

Not happening.

I had refused the Interstellar Brides testing protocols, not wanting to hope. Not daring to hope.

But fate had dropped my marked mate right into my lap. I knew she wanted to leave me, she'd made that blatantly clear. Why, I had yet to discover. But it wasn't because her body was cold to my touch. I saw need in her eyes when she looked at me, felt her pleasure when she came all over my cock. But with the need was also regret. Not for our connection, but for something else. Something I would discover.

My mate had secrets, but if she thought to walk away and keep those truths from me, she was sorely mistaken.

I was an Elite Hunter. There was nowhere in this universe she could go that I could not find her. Her scent was part of my cells, now. The sound of her voice the reason my heart beat. I could not lose her.

I wanted to toss her over my shoulder again and carry her off to my quarters, lock her in with me and never let her go. But that would not give me the answers I needed. She would not say, so I had to use my Hunter senses and discover the truth other ways.

I set down the recording equipment on the edge of a table and walked to the nearby table where my friends played their game.

Clearly, they were bored out of their minds, waiting for me as I neglected my duties to our people so I could play escort to a woman who couldn't wait to leave me.

"Kiel?" Lindsey's voice made me turn.

"Yes, mate?"

"Stop calling me that." Her hands were on her hips, her head tilted to the side as she scolded me. It was adorable. Perfect. So very Lindsey that I couldn't help but smile. Yes, the need to carry her off was strong.

"Never."

She blew her bangs out of her eyes and sighed. "Fine. Whatever. I'm all set up. Are you sure they're going to come?"

I nodded, turning to look at Kristin where she sat with her legs crossed in front of her on top of the table. She was too small to sit in the chairs, and she hated being so much shorter than everyone else. "Kristin? How many humans are on Base 3?"

She tossed a card into the middle of the table and raised her gaze to me. "Five since Brooks."

Behind me, Lindsey sighed. "Just five? Really? That's it?"

Kristin's gaze shifted to my mate, and the look in her eyes was neither welcoming nor hostile. Blank. Carefully blank. "There were six, before Brooks died. Eight, if you count me and Rachel."

Kristin unfolded her legs and walked over to Lindsey, standing eye-to-eye with my mate. "Where are you from?"

"Pittsburgh. You?"

"I was born in San Diego, but I was an Army brat. We moved every other year."

"I'm sorry."

Kristin shrugged. "I'm not."

"Where are you parents now?"

Kristin's shrug was even smaller. "Dead."

Lindsey froze, her hand stopping midway to the camera she was positioning for her interviews. "I'm so sorry."

"That's life. Lindsey, right?"

My mate nodded.

"We heard about you. Everyone's heard about you. We have to move on. Leave people behind. Adapt." The words were simple, and just what my mate needed to hear. Being a marked mate was new to me, too, but I would adapt. Unlike Lindsey, I wanted to do so. I wanted to make a life with her.

Lindsey's reaction was anything but...adaptable. She stiffened, her welcoming smile changing to something hard and brittle.

"Is that what you did? Adapt?"

Kristin tilted her head oddly, her eyes darker, more serious than I'd ever seen them. We'd only known each other a few months, both of us new to the planet, but we were close. We had to be to work together. But not close like Lindsey and me. Not close like Kristin and her Prillon mates.

Lindsey seemed hypnotized as Kristin spoke. "True love is a rare gift and I found it here." Her gaze darted to me, then back to my mate. "You can, too."

She shook her head once, definitively. "No."

"Why not?"

"I have to go home." Lindsey kept her hands busy, straightening the already perfectly positioned chair, adjusting the camera, checking the light.

"Why?" Kirstin lowered her voice. "Why? What's so important you have to get back? Are you married or something?"

I listened closely, honing all my senses to hear Lindsey's

answers. Kristin was asking the questions I wanted so badly to ask my mate, but knew she's shut down, turn me out.

"God, no." Lindsey's instant denial chilled my rage at even hearing the suggestion that she belonged to another. But she wouldn't look at me, wouldn't look at Kristin.

And gods be kind to Kristin Webster of Earth. I realized what she was doing now. She'd been an investigator on Earth, a member of an organization that hunted criminals, as I did. She was very, very good at asking questions, digging for answers, for the truth.

I remained still and quiet so she could continue.

Lindsey wiped tears from her cheeks and everything in me went on high alert. *What the fuck was going on with my mate?*

Part of me wanted to harm Kristin for making my mate feel any kind of sadness, but I stifled it. It wasn't Kristin wounding her, but whatever the fuck it was on Earth that held her. Pulled her back.

Fascinated, I watched the women interact. Something strange was going on here, but I didn't understand the nuances of human communication well enough to decipher their conversation.

Apparently, Lindsey had decided that was enough, that she would not offer more. She ignored Kristin and turned to me, her eyes overly bright, her smile too wide to be real. "Okay. Where are the five human soldiers? I'm ready."

Kristin met my gaze with a half smile and I nodded my thanks. She'd tried to break through Lindsey's walls, and I appreciated the effort. But if anyone was going to see into her soul, it was going to be me.

Kristen yelled to Rezzer to bring them in—Maxim had been swift with his orders to organize the interviews—and the giant Atlan walked to a smaller room and opened the door. The five human warriors living on Base 3 walked into the dining hall and took seats at the table across from my mate. Their odd collection of Hive implants and skin grafts, gadgets and silver flesh on display.

All of us wore the same battle armor. While it wasn't required—only Krael was the one to bring danger to us—it seemed we all felt more comfortable in the Coalition attire. It wasn't mentioned, but perhaps we were all prepared for harm to come to us again.

Lindsey introduced herself to wary, yet calm handshakes. It was not a custom on Everis, but since each male did it with Lindsey and Kristin didn't comment, it was a familiar action.

But not too familiar. None of them looked at Lindsey with a hint of heat. They held zero sexual interest in her. Curiosity, perhaps, at the Earth woman who'd arrived outside of protocol.

I watched my mate begin asking them her questions. She wanted to know everything about each warrior. Where he was born. Where he went to school. Why he volunteered for the Coalition Fleet, and how they ended up here. In hell.

My pride grew as she coaxed the men to talk about horrors none would willingly relive. If Kristin was good at intimidating people into answering her questions, Lindsey was a master at seducing their secrets from them. They told her everything, breaking down in tears, describing their capture and torture in detail as she watched them with those wide, compassionate eyes.

She touched them lightly. A hand on a wrist or shoulder. She touched them, held their hands in her own, comforted them...and I allowed it because I could see in them the same thing I felt when she touched me.

Peace. Acceptance. Hope where there had been none.

When she was done, they filed out in a quiet line, calmer than they had been. Perhaps relieved, even glad that their stories would be told. Was it because she was human that they'd shared, that she'd understood? While each one's story had varied, the basis was the same. They'd come from Earth, fought and had been captured. Tortured. Escaped. Brought here to live out their lives in whatever semblance of comfort they could find.

There was no difference in that because they were from Earth. No, my story was similar, almost identical. Same went probably for the Prillons and Atlans, too. Was what they shared enough for her? Would the men's stories be what she needed for those on Earth? Would it be enough to send back without her leaving?

Was the story *why* she was adamant about going home? No, home wasn't Earth for her any longer. Home was with me. I paced back and forth, breathed deeply.

Rezzer stalked over and sat in her interview chair, submitted to the same round of questions.

"What are you doing, Rezz?" I asked, confused. He wasn't from Earth. Far from it.

He looked from me to my mate and rubbed his huge hand over his head. "Telling the truth. They need to know what's out here. We need warriors to fight. We need brides to heal. Earth needs to do its part."

Rezz and Lindsey connected as she asked him about his home planet, Atlan. He partially shifted into beast mode for her, showed her what he was. Gave her his truth.

My mate was like a truth magnet. None seemed able to resist her lure, the soft safety and understanding offered in her green eyes.

Rezz was the last and Lindsey's shoulders slumped when she was done with her last question for him. The suns had set and the room had lost its warm glow. The interior lights were harsh and overly bright. She didn't meet my eyes and I could sense she was upset. Emotionally ragged. She tugged at the equipment to no avail, her movements awkward. Inefficient.

I came to her side, put my hand on top of hers. "Let me get that for you, mate."

"Don't." Tug. "Call." Tug. "Me." Tug. "That!" She yanked the camera piece from its dock and it flew back, taking her with it. I caught her before she could fall and pulled her to my chest. Tears streaked her face and I waved Kristin, Rezz and the others away with a flick of my wrist. They responded quickly and silently to settle at a table at the far side of the room. She'd respected their emotions, they'd respect hers.

"Shhh. I've got you." I offered comfort, but she wanted none. I wanted to give it to her, to hold her as she recovered herself.

"I didn't know. I had no idea what it was like out here." She sobbed, the hours of pain she'd just shared with the wounded warriors here obviously wore her down. She cried against my chest, wrapped her arms around me and clung tight as if she needed me.

I held her and I let her cry, put my cheek on top of her silky hair. It was my honor, my great privilege to be hers, to be her protector and comfort. Her soft heart and obvious concern for my brothers-in-arms made me fall even more in love with her. She was goodness and light, hope and healing. She touched the untouchable. Held their hands. Offered them solace when there was near to none to be had on this gods forsaken planet. She couldn't solve their problems, but she could listen to them, respect them.

"I never should have taken this stupid job." Her whisper was soft, but vehement.

Never taken this job? What the hell did that mean? She didn't want to be here? She never wanted to travel to the Colony. To meet me. To be with me.

"Why did you?" I asked.

"I—" She pulled away from me, wiping at her cheeks with stiff fingers. "Never mind. I have a headache."

If she was unwell, I would tend to her. It was a simple proof that I would cherish her. "Then I will take you to medical."

"Oh. No." She tried to push back, but I refused to let her out of the circle of my arms. "I didn't mean—"

"I insist." If my mate was in pain, the doctor would heal her. I lifted my hand and motioned my team closer once more. They rose as a group, came over silently. "I must take Lindsey to medical. Please be sure this equipment is sent to my quarters for Lindsey."

"Sure thing, boss," Kristin said.

"When do we return to the hunt?" Rezzer asked, hands on his hips. "The deep cavern sensors detected motion in section five twice in the last six hours."

That was news to me, and information that needed to be acted upon. Ever since we'd discovered Hive infiltrators on the Colony, and the traitor Krael had cost us the lives of half a dozen warriors, including Captain Brooks from Earth, we'd set up additional sensors, especially in the miles of natural caves that ran beneath the base. Every lead had to be investigated, even if my mate was now with me.

We couldn't afford to lose more men to the Hive. Every death brought down morale on the base. Our lives were bad enough without adding the threat of Hive capture back into the equation.

Rezz raised a brow and I knew he was right. It couldn't wait. If it turned out to be Hive, we put the entire planet at risk if we delayed. Yet I'd just found my marked mate and did not wish to leave her. I looked to Lindsey.

"What is it?" she asked.

"We have a traitor among us, the one who killed Captain Brooks. And others."

"And you have a lead?"

I nodded once. Out of the corner of my eye, I saw Rezz nod as well.

"Then you should go," she said. "I understand."

I had never been torn in two like this before. My instinctive need to Hunt was strong. Powerful. It had driven me my entire life with my complete focus. But now, my need to be with Lindsey was even greater. "I can't leave you like this."

"You can," she said. "You must. For Captain Brooks and the others. You must see justice done."

She understood, but that didn't make it any easier.

"Really," she added, placing her small hand on my arm. Her pale eyes held mine and I didn't see any wavering. "I'll be fine."

"I will take you to medical," I said, finding a compromise. "See that you are in good hands and then I will go."

"All right." I glanced to my team, who agreed. Except for Kristin, who responded very enthusiastically.

"Finally!" She bowed to Lindsey, and me. An apology for her outburst. "Sorry, it's just that I'm about to go stir-crazy. Tyran and Hunt seem to think I should spend less time at work and more time in bed."

Yes, I could understand her Prillons' interest in keeping their mate in bed and beneath them. That was all I wished to do with Lindsey.

Rezz laughed, the sound a deep booming chuckle that made my mate smile.

"Come, mate. I will see you well."

"Then you will go catch the bad guy."

I looked down at her, considered the Earth term. *Bad guy.*

"Yes, we will catch the bad guy and I will come back to you." I leaned in close, whispered in her ear. "And then I will make you scream my name."

CHAPTER 7

 indsey

"WHAT IS THAT?" I asked, my eyes following the blue wand Rachel waved in front of my face. The headache I had from hearing all of the men's stories, the horrors they'd faced at the hands of the Hive, had my head throbbing.

I sat upon an examination table in the medical wing of Base 3. Kiel had left me, grudgingly, but Rachel herself had assured him she'd take care of me and see me safely back to his quarters. Only then did he kiss me and leave.

Within seconds of the blue light moving back and forth, the pressure behind my left eye eased and the dull ache began to go away.

The Earth woman tended to me with a skepticism I recognized. In her green medical uniform and her brown hair pulled back into a ponytail, she was all business. I'd messed with her planet, with the safety of her mates and the others. While she didn't have children, she was very protective of everyone. Mated to the Governor, she saw one of her roles as guardian. I'd come and brought the possibility of harm to her people in a way she hadn't imagined. From a place she saw as hers as well. Earth was going to screw with The Colony and it was my fault. Or, at least, I was a tangible reminder of what could happen if the lies continued.

Yet, she was a biochemist. A very smart one, it seemed. She had more schooling than I would ever have. Years and years more. She was pragmatic, but she was also reasonable. I had no doubt I wasn't her favorite person, but she wasn't kicking me out either. It was because I was Kiel's mate, not because I was from Earth. Her alliance was to The Colony now.

She stopped moving it about, held it out to me. "It's a ReGen wand. There's a fancy, scientific explanation for what it does, but pretty much, it recognizes damaged cells and heals them."

I was afraid to reach out and take it, to hold it and study the tool that might be able to heal Wyatt.

"It can heal anything?"

"If you cut your arm off, no, it's not powerful enough." Her dark eyes held mine. "In Earth terms? Any major organ damage, probably not. Cuts, burns, broken bones. Pretty much anything an Urgent Care could tackle the wand can heal. Worse than that and you have to go in a ReGen Pod." She turned and pointed to a row of long, metal boxes. They were like the exam table I sat on, but each had what looked like a metal coffin on top. The lid was clear so whomever was inside could be easily seen.

"ReGen Pod?" I asked.

"ReGeneration Pod. Someone gravely injured goes in one of those. There's more blue light, much more healing power than the wand." She held it out for me and I took the small device.

"Can it heal cancer?"

"Yes."

"Diabetes?"

"Yes. Almost everything that people die from on Earth can be cured."

I hopped off the table, gripped the wand, paced. "Then why aren't these on Earth? Millions could be saved! Suffering —" I thought of Wyatt and the long days he'd cried in his hospital bed asking his mommy to make the pain go away. I'd held his hand and begged the nurses to drug him, to help him. But that was almost worse. His eyes would be glassy and he couldn't talk to me like a normal little boy. He was out of it, sleeping for so long I worried he might not wake up. Hot tears filled my eyes as I looked at this thing, not much bigger than my TV remote back home, and wanted to scream. "Why? It could help so many people."

Rachel sighed, leaned her hip against the side of the exam table. "True, but Earth isn't ready for this technology. Your presence here, your story is proof of that."

"Me?"

Rachel raised both brows. "It can heal, but it can also kill. Cause cancer. Create illness. Kill people and it would all look a hundred percent natural. Heart attack. Cancer. Strokes. Liver failure. Dementia. They could fry someone's brain just to make sure they forgot whatever it was they needed their victim to forget." She watched me for long minutes as I squirmed. "Do you honestly believe the governments and corporations on Earth would use this for good?"

I was a journalist. I wasn't exactly a globe-trotting war reporter, but I wasn't one to wear rose-colored glasses all the time either. As a single mother I didn't have that luxury. No, the news fed a steady diet of corruption and war. Murder and terrorism. Rachel was right. The Coalition was right. But that just made my heart burn in my chest. Everyone would suffer because the greedy and corrupt, the evil on Earth had not been eradicated or controlled.

"Humans truly are savages."

Rachel sighed, and the sound nearly broke my heart. "Yes. We really are."

"But I need it. So many people are suffering. Can't you sneak one back and not tell anyone? Give it to someone trustworthy? I'd never tell a soul, I swear. I'd destroy it as soon as I was—" I thought of Wyatt and waved the wand in the air. "This? This little thing could save my—"

I pinched my lips together, turned away. Tears spilled down my cheeks and I frantically wiped them away. I'd said too much, but my emotions, my need to heal Wyatt made me fierce. I'd do anything for him, even beg this human woman who didn't like me much for help.

"Save your what, Lindsey?" Rachel asked. For the first time, her voice was missing that hard edge.

I didn't reply.

"You're not an investigative journalist. No offense, but they're sneaky. Ruthless. Mean. Hard." Her hand came to rest on top of my shoulder and the gentle touch made me jump as she continued. "You're none of those things. I mean, you were discovered at the fighting pits. The entire base is talking about the way Kiel fought for you. No one trying to be sneaky gets exposed like that."

I laughed at my own stupidity. "Well, I am a journalist and a blogger. It's just that I usually don't work on this kind of story. I'm more the hospital benefit, parenting articles kind of writer. So, yeah, I'm pretty bad at being a spy."

"Why are you really here?"

I turned to face her. "To get the truth. To find out what happened to Captain Brooks. His uncle is a Senator. He was from a rich, powerful family that thinks the Coalition is lying about what's going on up here. So, they sent me. *That* is the truth."

Rachel's eyes were serious, but not hard. "I was a whistle-blower. I discovered the CEO of the company I worked for was putting out bad medicine and it was killing people. I reported it and because of that, was set up to take the fall. I was convicted to twenty-five years in jail."

My mouth fell open. Holy shit.

"I chose to be an Interstellar Bride and was matched and sent here instead of going to prison. I found the truth, shared it and it was used against me. They made me the patsy and I took the fall. It wasn't used for good. How can you guarantee what you've learned here won't be used to make things worse for The Colony?"

"I'll do everything I can to make sure that won't happen."

She arched a brow. "You know all about spin, Lindsey. Think about it. You can't stop them. These guys need hope. They need brides. And what you're doing is going to destroy everything. Since Brooks died, we've only had one bride. *One.* In months. How can you make sure whatever you take back won't be used to scare people away from the Coalition? From the Brides Program?"

"Because...because I know what it's like, what you guys are doing. I know about Krael and the Hive and—"

"Yes, but they could spin everything you give them for political gain. Sacrifice lives for money. Just as it happened to me. A big pharmaceutical company put money above people's lives. God, the warriors here on The Colony want to live. They want love, family, children. They are barely clinging to hope, holding on by their fingernails. If you're going to share something with Earth, share that we need more Brides. More volunteers to come here and find their perfect match."

I bit my lip. That wasn't what the people who hired me wanted, and I knew it. But could I go through with this now?

I had to. They'd hurt Wyatt if I didn't. But sacrifice the happiness of everyone here on the Colony? That was a horrible choice. A terrible burden. And the weight of it was crushing me. I couldn't breathe. I curled my hands around the edge of the exam table, my knuckles turning white as I stared at a smudge on the otherwise pristine floor. Focus. I just needed to breathe.

Rachel yelling at me didn't help. She was really angry, her cheeks bright red and her hands in fists at her side, as if she were ready to punch me in the nose.

I deserved it. But Wyatt didn't deserve what was going to happen to him if I didn't go home and give Senator Brooks and his people what they wanted.

Rachel's voice rose in volume and I winced, my headache back in full force. "But no. It's not about that for you. What are you after, Lindsey? Money? Right? You get to buy a new car and all the warriors here get to die a little more inside every damn day. Tell me I'm wrong? Tell me you're not some selfish, stupid little girl willing to ruin all their lives for nothing more than a few more zeros in your bank account. Money, right? That's why you're so desperate to get this story and go home."

I couldn't deny it. If I did, I'd have to tell her the truth. "Seems like you've got me all figured out." I sniffed, lifted my chin and looked straight at her with the tears pooling in my eyes. She was a warped blur on the other side of those stinging tears. "You think you're so smart. Keep talking."

She offered me a small smile, crossed her arms. "Everyone's asked why you're here. Everyone else believes your story." She walked to the wall, to a small table and brought back a soft cloth. "Wipe away those tears, Lindsey, and tell me what's really going on. It's just us. No one else is around.

You're Kiel's mate. That means you're mine now, too. Kiel is a good man, and he's suffered enough. Tell me why you're really here. Let me help you. Let Maxim help you. Prime Nial is my husband's friend. He's mated to a human, too. Her name is Jessica. She'll help you, too. You just have to tell me the truth."

We were in a second room of the medical unit. While there were some doctors and technicians in the other room, Rachel had claimed this space for privacy. Now I knew why she wanted it. She was whispering now and I took the small white cloth and wiped my eyes as she whispered. "Why are you here?"

I took a deep breath. Let it out. My gut made the decision to trust her. My heart was talking before my brain could catch up. There was just something fierce about Rachel, something strong. I trusted her to help me.

"My son. His name is Wyatt and he's three."

Her dark eyes widened. "You have a son?"

I choked on a sob and took a deep breath, trying to suck in strength like air. "A little over three months ago, we were in a car accident. I came out with just cuts and bruises, but even in his car seat, Wyatt was hurt. His leg. It was broken, cut, destroyed. They patched him up, did a couple surgeries, but couldn't *fix* him. The growth plate was damaged and is fusing early. His leg is going to stop growing. They want to do surgery to try to help, but it's not good."

Rachel remained quiet as I spoke.

"He needs more surgery. More than the ones he's had. And if they can't fix it, he's going to have to have surgery and bone grafting as he grows for the rest of his life. My crap insurance denied the surgery as not medically necessary, which is total bullshit. I am trying to appeal, but... there's no money." I laughed but there was no joy in the sound, only despair. I looked her in the eye and told her the rest. "There's no money to pay for the ones he's already had."

"And the Senator offered you a lot of money to come here and get this story?"

I nodded. "Yes. Enough to take care of Wyatt. And I can't stay here. I can't be a bride, a mate. I have a son. I'm a mother." My shoulders were shaking, but I held the cry of pain inside. "Kiel is wonderful. Amazing. God—I can't describe—" I stuttered, but Rachel was nodding. She understood the pull of mates since she had two. Two! She knew what leaving would cost me. "I—I can't leave my son. Not even for him."

"Your son. Without the surgeries now, he'll be crippled for life?"

I nodded, the tears streaming down my face in silent agony. Now that I'd shared the truth, I couldn't hold back the pain. "I want the money, but...but I want this ReGen thing more." I held up the device that was like a magic wand. I waved it about. "This would heal him. Within minutes."

I slid off the exam table and forced back the tears. I looked Rachel in the eye and held the wand up between us. "I have to go. Take this back to him. Heal him. I don't care about the story. I never did."

"They'll be waiting for you," she said. "Wanting the story. The video, audio. They won't pay you without it."

"I don't want the money!" I shouted, waving the wand. "I want this."

"I give you the wand and I keep your story?"

Yes, she was protective. And shrewd. And ridiculously cautious. I couldn't blame her, not after what had happened to her on Earth.

"I have to give them something." My voice shook. "They'll hurt him if I don't."

"Nice people." Rachel studied me closely, but didn't snatch

the wand away. Going over to a wall, she swiped her finger over the glossy black. It came alive with all kinds of colors and words, shapes and numbers. After a few more swipes, a screen appeared that displayed the Interstellar Brides Program logo.

"I'm not going to be a bride," I said.

"You don't need to be. You're already mated to Kiel."

"Oh god," I murmured, my heart breaking all over again. "Kiel."

She turned away from the wall display and faced me. "You will return to Earth, to your son, Wyatt, and walk away from your marked mate?"

"Can he come with me?"

She shook her head. "No. Earth won't even take back its own soldiers who've been contaminated by Hive tech. They'll never agree to allow an alien to live there. I mean, Kiel wouldn't exactly blend in."

"Can Wyatt live here? Can Maxim or the Prime you were talking about get Wyatt permission to live here?" I was grasping at straws, but maybe there was a chance we could all be together. I knew the rules, but hoped one could be bent...for me.

"No." She bit her bottom lip, her eyes filling with tears in an apparent display of empathy. "That's an Earth rule, not a Coalition one. They will allow full grown adults to make the decision to become a citizen of another world and give up citizenship. But a child? No. They're not allowed to make that decision until they come of age. And no adult is allowed to make it for them."

She killed any hope I might have felt. "So I'm screwed. I have to choose between Kiel and my son."

"Yes." She wiped a tear off her cheek. "It appears that way. You've made your choice. Are you really willing to give up your marked mate to return to your child?"

"It's not like a have a choice." The words fell from my lips in a whisper.

"Yes, you do." Rachel closed her eyes and held them closed for long moments, as if my pain were her own. "It's a sucky choice, but it is a choice. Are you sure? Maybe we can figure something out?"

I felt the weight of the question pressing on me. It was like an elephant. Oppressive and squashing me like a bug. I had to choose between the only man in the universe for me and my son. I couldn't have both. There was no question as to my choice. While it would feel as if my arm was ripped off by leaving Kiel behind, it was Wyatt who needed me more.

"I can't leave him alone. I can't abandon him." The tears came in earnest and I sobbed. "He's my baby. I can't—"

Rachel's face transformed then. Every hard edge, every calculating gleam was gone. She had to use both hands to wipe wet cheeks as she turned back to the screen. "Then we must get you back before Prime Nial forces you to stay. You might choose your son, but I can't guarantee the Prime won't choose to protect his own people, the warriors who fought for him."

"Are you kidding me?" *Prime Nial*—

"I don't know. I doubt they've ever faced this problem before. But are you willing to take the chance?"

"No." I wasn't. No question. Wyatt needed me. I'd made him a promise that I would return to him, and I intended to keep it.

The screen buzzed for a moment as the link connected and a familiar face appeared. Rachel greeted the woman whose stern face filled the screen. "Warden Egara."

"Rachel," the Earth warden responded. "Miss Walters."

The mate of the Governor of Base 3 spoke, her voice clear and determined. "We need your help."

CHAPTER 8

*L*indsey

GOD, I was an emotional mess.

It had taken thirty frustrating minutes, but I'd figured out how to adjust the window tinting in Kiel's quarters. I was now able to look out upon the rocky terrain, see the rugged beauty of the planet. While the room was temperature controlled, I shivered and I rubbed my arms.

I'd gone into this little adventure into outer space with only one thing on my mind. Wyatt. While I didn't think any less often of him, I'd been surprised—no, stunned—by what I'd come to learn. The Colony wasn't some prison. It wasn't some outer space outpost of heathens. These were warriors who'd fought for the Coalition, been brave and courageous, even when captured by the Hive. Tortured. Altered. Forever changed.

Yet when it was time to go home, back to the families and people they'd fought so hard to protect, they weren't

welcome. Rejected by their own people as being dangerous
and damaged. Broken.

Despite it all, they were on the Colony building new lives, a
new world. They could have been lawless, like a weird *Mad Max*
movie, but they were honorable warriors, not just from Earth,
but from all the Coalition worlds. I'd met Rezzer the Atlan and
he'd transformed into his beast for me, on camera, and under
complete control. The memory sent a shiver of adrenaline
through my body. The sharp-featured warriors with the golden,
brown and copper coloring were from the main planet, the
people in charge of the whole Fleet, the Prillons from Prillon
Prime. They were huge, but had been nothing but courteous to
me. The two Prillon that were friends with Kiel, Captain Marz
and Lieutenant Vance, fought in the war for fourteen years.

That was more than half my life.

They gave me access to video records of Hive battles and
I *saw* what those things were. And here, on the Colony, I was
surrounded by what they did. Hurt people. Torture their
captives. Change their bodies into something no longer
human, or Prillon, or Atlan, no longer safe.

Contaminated. That was the word I heard over and over
from the human men I interviewed. They looked frightening,
something straight out of sci-fi movie with silver skin and
circuitry built into their flesh. One of them had two
completely silver eyes. He was dark skinned, from Atlanta
and his mother had named him Denzel after her favorite
actor. Now his close cut, curly black hair and dark skin
surrounded eyes that looked like liquid mercury.

Seeing him cry had almost broken me in half. He had two
sisters and a mother who'd raised all three of them on her
own. She'd screamed and cried when he'd called her on the
video screen to tell her why he could never come home
again.

A very religious woman, she'd taken one look at his eyes, called him a demon and told him to kill himself.

And that wasn't even the worst I'd heard. Seemed it didn't matter what planet these guys were from, no one wanted them back. Everyone was afraid. Their people were afraid of them. Their governments were afraid of them. According to Kiel, that fear was not without merit.

One bad frequency generator could reactivate all of their Hive technology. The implants were literally dormant, waiting to be turned back on. And some of the men had the Hive implants in their brains. Their spines. According to Rezzer, the Prillon named Tyran, one of Kristin's mates, had so much Hive technology in his muscles that he was actually stronger than the Atlan in full beast mode.

Scary was an understatement.

But they'd all been kind to me. In fact, the two people on this planet with the worst attitudes were the two human women, Rachel and Kristin. They both looked at me like I was torturing their favorite pet. They were so protective, so determined to save these guys, to give them some kind of happiness. Hope. Their mates had been tortured and broken, and now the women were determined to save them. To see other brides come to The Colony.

Senator Brooks had been wrong. Very wrong. Why shouldn't he have been? No one knew the whole truth. I did. But I was here on the planet. I was supposed to be an observer. A *hidden* observer.

Yeah, that had lasted all of five minutes just as Rachel had said. I was a horrible investigator. But I'd gotten involved with these people. Learned the real stories. The truth. That's what they wanted back on Earth. Well, that's what they *claimed* to want, but I couldn't guarantee these guys that their stories wouldn't be spun into lies. I hadn't cared when I was on the transport shuttle. I hadn't cared about anything but making Wyatt better. Safe.

But now I cared about more than just my son. I cared about the warriors here. I cared about Kiel. He'd refused to be interviewed, but I didn't need to put him in front of a camera and pester him with questions to know he was a good man. I felt it when our minds touched in the dreams. I felt it when he touched *me*.

Kiel.

He'd been unexpected. Yeah, I'd longed for someone to be mine. I longed for a man who was trustworthy, protective, honorable and brave. Caring and thoughtful. Even a little wicked and a whole lot dirty. But I never would have found *him* on Earth. No, he'd been waiting for me here. And he wanted me. Said I was destined to be his. Me!

The mark on my palm was now quiet. It didn't hurt any longer, but my heart ached now, that pain exponentially worse. I'd spent one night with my marked mate—God, I couldn't even wrap my head around that truth—and I wanted more. I wanted a lifetime. I didn't have to know him for months to know that he was the one for me. The. One.

I'd go back to Earth and search the entire planet and I would never find a man more perfect for me than Kiel.

He was mine. My complete match.

It wasn't kismet or serendipity. No, we'd been marked. Matched by fate, or God, or some unknown and unseen force that had somehow marked my palm and his—even though we were born clear across the universe from one another.

Kiel, the Hunter from Everis, was mine.

But I was leaving. Going back to Earth and choosing Wyatt over him. I would choose Wyatt over everything. While Kiel was my marked mate, Wyatt was my *son*. I could never walk away from him, never abandon him.

Nothing would keep me from him, not even true love with an unexpected and wonderful alien warrior, or ten light years of cold, black, empty space.

Rachel was helping me transport home. She'd shared her truth, ensured I knew it and would take it with me in the hopes that if women on Earth heard what she had to say, more brides would come to the Colony. She only wanted these warriors happy. While not everyone wanted a mate, most probably did. A family, children. Love.

Rachel, as it turned out, was pretty amazing. She knew my truth, knew the reason I would leave Kiel behind. I couldn't tell him. No. He wouldn't let me go. According to Rachel, he literally would not be able to allow me to leave. His need was beyond human, an instinct in the core of his being that would never allow him to leave me, no matter the circumstances.

Only death was strong enough to tear him from my side.

But he didn't have a son with trusting blue eyes and dimples. He'd never felt the soft sweetness of chubby little arms squeezing his neck, sloppy wet kisses on his cheek, and the whispered confession of 'I love you, mommy' in the middle of the night.

I stood still and fought the tears welling beneath my eyelids like liquid fire. *Wyatt.*

I had to go home.

That was why, when Kiel came into his quarters, I leapt to my feet, then leapt onto him wrapping my legs around his waist. I had to walk away from him, let him go, but not right now. Not until Warden Egara said.

Soon though. Too soon, so I would make the most of the time I had left. I'd never been so aroused, so eager for a man as I was with Kiel. Even though he was from Everis, from another planet, he was *all* man. The way his shoulders felt wide and solid beneath my palms, his waist trim and firm under my wrapped legs, his rippling belly pressed against my mound, his bulging cock nudging against my eager pussy. One hundred percent pure, unadulterated man. And he was all mine.

For tonight.

"Well, hello," he said, the corner of his mouth tipping up.

"Did you find him? Krael?"

Kiel's face hardened. "No. But we will. I'll be called out again soon." He looked at me, stroked his knuckles over my cheek and I watched as his tension eased. "In the meantime, is there something you want?"

"Yes." I wiggled my hips, brushing more firmly against his cock. "I want you naked."

His chest rumbled with a very primitive, manly sound. "The mark makes us hot for each other. It keeps us...very eager until the claiming is done."

I leaned in, ran my lips along the length of his neck, felt the slight rasp of his beard, breathed in his clean, dark scent. "I thought that was what we did last night." I bit lightly at the tendon in his neck.

His big hands gripped my bottom, hoisted me up as he carried me to the bed.

Putting a knee on the bed, he lowered me down, even as I kept my hold. Looked up into his dark brown eyes. "A formal claiming ceremony is when I make you mine, Lindsey. I'll fill you with my cock, fill you with my seed as our marks touch. Then, and only then, will we be joined forever."

He'd fucked me the night before. More than once. I'd had his cum slipping from me all day, but I couldn't remember him ever clasping our fingers together, making our palms touch.

I felt the desperate urge to say yes, to do just that. To make him mine. Forever. But that wasn't to be. That would be selfish of me. Worse, cruel. If we were bound forever, he'd never be able to get over me or find someone else, another woman, to love him.

The very idea was like a dagger in my heart, but I would not deny him happiness, even if it couldn't be with me. Kiel very much deserved to be loved.

He frowned, slid a hand up my body so he cupped my cheek. Looked at me. *Really* saw me. "What's wrong? Why are you sad?"

I swallowed hard, forced the lump of tears lodged in my throat back down. I wasn't going to cry. I couldn't let him know that I was upset, that this was the last time I'd be beneath him, that I'd feel his heat, his breath, his cock. His kiss.

"Nothing. Kiss me."

I saw his dimple form just before he lowered his head and did as I bid. His mouth was warm and firm. Gentle.

Too gentle.

I moved my hands to the back of his head, tugged at his thick, dark hair. I didn't want to tell him this was the last time we'd be together, that I wanted to make the most of every second of it, but I'd show him.

At my insistence, he changed the kiss. Yes, I'd initiated and even showed him what I wanted, but I let him lead. I liked that he was in charge. Either he was ridiculously skilled —which I didn't want to think too deeply about—or the mark made him naturally in tune with what made me hot. He knew how to kiss me, the way to tangle his tongue with mine. The way to touch me. And soon, god, and soon, the way to fuck me.

My ankles were still crossed at the small of his back. Propped up on one forearm, his free hand roamed over me from neck to hip before he growled. "You have too many clothes on."

Only at the idea of getting naked did I place my feet on the bed by his hips.

"You first," I told him.

While he lifted one dark brow, he remained silent as he tucked his fingers beneath the hem and tugged his armored shirt up and over his head, letting it fall to the floor at the foot of the bed.

Lifting my hands, I roamed over the broad expanse of heated skin, felt the rock hard muscles play beneath my palms. I bit my lip, ran my fingertips over the flat disk of a nipple, heard his quick intake of breath.

My eyes lifted to his, saw the heated pools had turned almost black. I knew he was on a short leash with his control —I felt the same.

"You're not finished," I added.

"If I take them off, we'll be done too soon."

The idea that I'd pushed him to the edge, that he was ready to come from just kissing me, from my hands on his bare chest made me feel powerful. I'd never had this much control over someone before. I'd never felt this wanted, this desired.

I reached for his pants, began to undo the button there. His hands covered mine, looked at me. "I want to see you. Taste you. I haven't done that yet. I want to swallow you down."

"You are a dangerous woman."

I shook my head, my hair sliding over the soft blanket. "I'm not. I just want you."

"I can deny you nothing, mate."

That word brought me pain now, but I ignored it and focused on watching him, in memorizing the heated look in his eyes, the power and grace with which he moved. I needed to sear him into my mind like he was now. Aroused. Strong.

Mine.

Pushing off, he moved to stand at the foot of the bed, toed off one boot, then the other, before shucking his pants. Coming up onto my knees, I watched as every single inch of his perfect body was exposed.

His cock...it was a glorious thing. Big. So big. Thick and long. It was a fleshy red, smooth with a bulging vein running along the side. The flared head was bulbous and darker, pointed straight at me and the little slit oozed a bit of pre-cum. I licked my lips, eager for a taste. Reaching out, I grasped the base, my fingers not able to close all the way around the hot flesh.

"Wow." Even though I'd been fucked with that...that beast the night before, I hadn't had this much time to ogle it.

"That's all for you, mate."

His grin set me at ease and I leaned forward to lick up the pearly drop of fluid. His breath hissed out and his hips bucked at the slightest touch. He was so tall I didn't have to stoop far. We were at almost the perfect height for me to take him into my mouth.

But a finger on my chin had me looking up.

"If you're going to suck me off, I want you naked when you do it."

It was my turn to strip down. While I'd packed a small bag for travel, including only a second Coalition fighter uniform, I had several pair of my undies. Kiel had been so into the ones I'd worn the day before, I wasn't going to wear any standard issue underpants now. I had no idea what they looked like, but I wanted to see Kiel's desire again.

So my lacy pale pink bra and panty set was revealed as I took off the standard uniform. I didn't have double-D breasts, so what I did have, I liked to make pretty. As I reached behind my back to undo the clasp, he put a hand on my upper arm to still me.

His gaze raked over my body as he spoke. "Wait. I want to

look at you." His hand came up and stroked over the delicate fabric at the curve of my breast. "What's this called?"

I looked down at myself, at the blunt fingertips, dark and masculine beside my milk pale breast and bra.

"Lace?" I asked.

One fingertip ran gently over the floral pattern. "Lace," he replied, as if testing out the word. "Besides you, this is what I like from Earth the most."

Yes, I could see the way his cock pulsed and bobbed before me, he liked it a whole heck of a lot.

"Do you want me to take it off?"

Slowly, he shook his head, but ran his finger over my nipple and watched as it beaded into a hard point.

Only when he pulled his hand away did I lower my head again, this time taking him fully into my mouth, the size of him stretching my jaw as I worked the base of his cock with my hand, squeezing and twisting as I sucked on the head.

He groaned and his hands tangled in my hair.

The salty tang of his pre-cum coated my tongue as I licked and laved him, moving over him deeper and deeper each time. I wasn't a porn star, so I had a gag reflex and couldn't take him as far as I wanted. But the way he was tugging on my hair and breathing hard, I knew I was doing something right.

"I'm close, mate. Swallow me down."

Yes. I wanted to taste him, to know his true flavor. Perhaps it was because we were marked mates that I thought this way or just because I'd turned into a horny slut on a strange planet. I didn't care. I just wanted to make him come. I needed to feel powerful, and I wanted to feel like I'd given him something, brought him pleasure. It was a selfish desire, a way to ease my conscience at what I knew was coming. I was going to hurt him, and that knowledge made me all the more determined to please him now.

If only Earth didn't have such strict restrictions on their Interstellar Brides Program. I was a single mother, I had a child, which meant I couldn't volunteer.

Stupid rule. Stupid, stupid rule.

But then, before meeting Kiel, volunteering for the program had never even crossed my mind.

And now it was too late. I loved him, but I had to leave him behind.

Sliding my grip up and down, I worked his entire length. He groaned one last time, his hips shifting forward as he shouted out my name. His cock swelled, then pulsed, the hot seed splashing on the back of my tongue. Quickly, I swallowed again and again to take it all.

Only when I felt his body relax did I pull back. Using the back of my hand, I wiped my mouth. His big hand cupped my jaw again and I looked up into his dark eyes.

I only had a second to see the pleased, and very sated, look on his face before he lifted me up and tossed me across the bed. I bounced once on my back as I gasped in surprise. He was on me between one blink and the next. I remembered how fast he moved during the challenge and he used it when he saw fit and damn if that didn't make me so fucking hot I could barely breathe.

With his knees and forearms on either side of me, caging me in, he pinned me with his gaze.

"My turn, mate." His voice was husky, as if he was overcome with emotion. He leaned down and kissed me softly. "All night. I'm going to fuck you all night. I'm going to make you scream my name."

All night? Yes, please. I looked down his body, saw that his cock might have been sated, but it was still rock hard. He dropped his head so he looked between our bodies, then back at me. Grinned wickedly.

"I am always like this, now that I have found you."

"Wow."

"Your turn." He slid down my body, his palms stroking a heated path to my thighs, where he pushed them apart and settled himself so there was no way I was going to close my legs.

"This lace," he commented, a finger running over the dainty edge of my panties at the seam of my thigh. His warm breath fanned my sensitive skin and made me very aware of what he was about to do. Yet he took his time to be... in awe. He was too damn patient.

All night. I wasn't going to survive if he planned to taunt me like this *all night.*

"It is very delicate and does not do much to cover you."

It didn't. My butt cheeks were barely covered by the thin material and the little strings at the side were all that kept them up. They certainly weren't any kind of barrier from *him.*

Lowering his head, he ran his tongue over the wet material. Nope. No barrier at all.

I gasped at the heat of just that simple touch. Then the tip of his finger hooked the fabric, slid it to the side so my pussy was visible and his tongue flicked over me again. "Much better. Now I can taste you. Breathe in your sweet scent."

My hips moved of their own volition as he learned my folds and found my clit.

I cried out his name.

"I like hearing my name upon your lips."

His hands came up, tugged the sides of my panties and carefully lowered them down. "These are too pretty to rip."

I shifted so he could work them down my legs and off. He returned to his spot between my thighs and he didn't hold back any longer. With his thumbs, he opened me up so all of me was visible. With a ruthless grace, he worked me with his tongue. I couldn't keep my hips still, but he put one palm on my lower belly to hold me in place. Of course, that didn't do much good when he slipped two fingers of his other hand inside of me. He curled them over my g-spot and I spiraled tight, so close to shattering.

He must have sensed it because he stilled, lifted his head.

I looked down my body at him. "Why did you stop?" I asked breathlessly. "I want to come."

His lips were coated with my arousal. "All night, mate."

Curling his fingers again, I pushed up so I was on my elbows. I had a sexy alien between my legs and I wanted him there. Two days ago I never would have imagined such a thing. Now? Now I had to make this last, to remember every sly smile, every stroke of his finger, every flick of his tongue because they would be my last. This was my last night with him and I wanted it all.

I nodded. "All night."

I flopped back down on the bed and let him have his way with me. Fortunately, this time when he lowered his head again, he didn't taunt me. No, he found the spot on my clit that made me cry out and clench my thighs around his head and pushed me to the brink, then over.

Colors swirled behind my eyelids as I screamed. With my thighs over his ears, I had no doubt the sound was muffled for him. But he knew I was coming. My pussy flooded with my juices, my inner walls clenching and squeezing his fingers. When had I tangled my fingers in his hair?

With one gentle kiss on my clit, he came up over me. I opened my eyes, saw him smirking, quite pleased with himself.

"That's one."

I was too relaxed to do more than frown. "One?"

"Orgasm. You're going to have many of them."

"Oh god," I whispered, my eyes falling closed. My skin

was damp with sweat, my pussy tingling and swollen, but I ached for his cock. "More."

I was such a slut with him—I'd never behaved this way before—but I wanted more orgasms. I wanted so many I blacked out.

Lowering his hips, he brushed his cock over slick flesh, the contact making me whimper.

"Is that what you want?"

I nodded my head.

He slid in an inch, stilled.

"More?"

I opened my eyes, met his, nodded again. "More."

He slid in another inch.

"Kiel!" I cried in exasperation. I slid my hands from his lower back and over the flexing muscles of his butt, tried to pull him into me. Shifting my knees, I adjusted so he could go even deeper.

"You're not in control here, mate. I am. Your pleasure is mine. It's my honor and privilege to give it to you."

"Then give it to me now," I whined. His flared head stretched me open and I wanted more. I wanted deeper. I wanted all of him.

"Bossy thing, aren't you?" With one deep plunge, he filled me completely. I gasped, arched my head back. "Like that?"

"Yes," I breathed.

He pulled back until just the crown held me open, then drove deep again. I was wet, so very wet that I could hear it. This wasn't tame sex. This wasn't a quickie. This was raw, dirty, powerful.

"Yes," I repeated, starting a chant that matched his motions until I was shifting to take him, to take it all. Until I came.

I was a sweaty, weak, sated mess. When I had the strength to open my eyes, I saw him grinning, proud of his virility and ability to please his mate. His cock was still hard and he had the calm focus of a man who was far from coming.

His focus on me was laser sharp. He'd given me one orgasm and the way he started to move his hips again, he was prepared to give me one more.

"All night, mate," he vowed, reaching down and rubbing his thumb gently over my already sensitive clit. "Forever."

I whimpered, knowing I was completely at his—and his cock's—mercy. All night, yes. Forever? Impossible. I pushed that thought from my mind and let him rule my body, because come morning, I'd be gone.

So I gave over to him. All. Night. Long.

I let what this *thing* was between us consume me.

CHAPTER 9

*L*indsey, *Interstellar Brides Processing Center, Miami, Two Hours Earlier*

THE TRANSPORT PAD was still humming when I stumbled off the smooth black surface and into Warden Egara's arms.

"Slow down. Give yourself a minute. You just traveled through space." Her normally stern voice was calm and soothing. Too calm.

"Let me go." I shook off the arm she'd wrapped around my waist and headed out the doors to the employee area where the people I worked for had taken me before. Without the warden's knowledge, of course. There was a locker room in the back where the cafeteria and cleaning staff kept their personal belongings and my things should still be there. My clothes. My cell phone. All in hiding awaiting my return.

I needed to call my mom, warn her to bundle Wyatt up and meet me somewhere other than home. Somewhere safe. Anywhere else but the run down old apartment building we'd lived in the last couple years.

"Lindsey, look at me." Warden Egara barked at me but I waved her away, patting down the uniform and pants I still wore. They were green. Rachel dressed me up like a medical officer and shoved the ReGen wand in my pocket before I left the Colony. The Colony. God, I was in a familiar place, home on Earth, and yet I felt nauseated, literally sick knowing that Kiel was so far away. My mark no longer felt warm. It was dead now. Nothing more than colored skin. I missed the heat, the warm, pulsing connection to my mate. To the man I loved.

No, my mark wouldn't let me forget Kiel. He was seared into my brain, part of me now, just as the mark was part of my hand.

But I was home and close to Wyatt. So close. All I had to do was get to him before Senator Brooks and his crazy conspiracy crowd.

The pants and tunic were comfortable enough, and I sighed in relief when I felt the bulge of the ReGen wand in the pants pocket. If this wand healed Wyatt as it should, the trip had been worth it. The heartache that would follow me the rest of my life would be worth it. I sucked in a deep breath and clenched my fist hoping to ease the ache of knowing the connection between was dead. "I have to go."

Jogging to the locker rooms, the warden ran behind. I ignored her. I didn't care about her. I only cared about one person, one thing.

Wyatt.

A minute later I stood in front of an open locker and tore the alien clothing from my body. Shimmying into my comfy jeans and cotton t-shirt, I yanked my mommy-sized purse from the hook and shoved the ReGen wand inside. When I sat down to slide my feet into my sandals, the warden grabbed my bag and I froze. The healing wand was in that bag. I needed that wand for Wyatt.

I pounced, tugged at the strap of the bag. "What are you doing?"

"Do I have your attention?"

"Absolutely." She released the bag, let me take it. Sitting back down on the bench, I tucked it beside me—at my side and away from her.

I slipped my feet into the sandals and tensed, ready to fight for the bag again if necessary. No one was stealing the wand from me now. I was on Earth, with the healing wand and Wyatt was so close. *Healing* him was so close. The warden might look tough, but I was desperate. I'd claw her eyes out if I had to. Anything for Wyatt. Anything, including leaving Kiel behind.

"You are to take the wand, heal your son, and return it to me immediately. Do you understand? I'm breaking about a hundred rules letting you take it out of this building, rules that could cost me my job."

Okay. Yeah. She had a point. She'd risked a lot to help me. So had Rachel, including the wrath of her two mates. Right now, she was probably taking a lot of heat for me.

"I'm sorry. I understand, and I promise I'll bring it back as soon as I heal Wyatt's leg. I give you my word."

"And no one else can see it, or know it exists. This technology is forbidden on Earth. It doesn't *exist* here."

"I promise. I swear, I'll do exactly what you said. I just need to heal Wyatt's leg." I reached for the handle of the purse. It was hard and round, like a curved piece of bamboo in my grip. But the warden didn't grab for it again.

Dressed and ready to go, I dug through the contents until I found my phone. I turned it on, waiting impatiently for the operating system to reboot. The battery was still fully charged. I'd only been gone a couple of days, but God, it felt like a lifetime.

I wasn't the same person I'd been when I left. I was

stronger now. Loving Kiel had made me stronger somehow. Braver. I would heal Wyatt and dupe the assholes who sent me to the Colony. Hopefully, the warden had enough time to take care of the second half of Rachel's plan.

"Did Rachel send you the files?" I asked.

Warden Egara nodded, her smile a bit wider this time. "Yes."

"And? Did you have enough time?"

"I had to call in some help, but yes. We have all the files fully edited and up online. We also sent copies to the major news agencies, so they should be broadcasting any time now."

The broken little part of me that had been withering and dying at the thought of betraying the warriors of the Colony warmed and healed. Rezzer and Marz, the governor and the others, the humans I'd talked to, would have their story told. The truth. Not some bullshit spin-doctored version of things used to stir up trouble for the warriors on the Colony.

I was done being a pawn.

The warden and Rachel wanted to use the interviews I'd done, the personal stories of the warriors to try to recruit brides who might ask to be assigned to the Colony. I didn't know how the Interstellar Brides program worked, exactly, but the warden had insisted that if a woman actually requested a certain planet, she would not be denied.

And the Colony needed more brides. Rachel had said that often enough, but I agreed. I saw the warriors. Met them. They needed hope and life and children running around. They needed noise and chaos and a future. They needed to remember what they'd sacrificed and fought for in the first place. And it wasn't the bleak, shadow of existence they had now. Things were improving, but not fast enough for Rachel. She wanted everyone on the Colony happy. Now.

Except for Kiel. He wouldn't be matched. He wouldn't

have his mate at his side. I'd denied him the happiness he deserved, the kind of relationship he couldn't find with anyone else. I'd doomed Kiel to live an empty life by choosing to save my son. By lying to him, leaving him behind. I hadn't even said goodbye.

"They should let single mothers into the brides program," I whispered. "Because this sucks."

The warden nodded, a shimmer of moisture gathering in her eyes in empathy for my pain. "I agree. But that's an Earth rule, not a Coalition rule."

"It's stupid."

"Earth's leaders don't feel that the choice to travel to another world can be made for a minor. They can't go until they are old enough to make their own decision."

I knew the rules. At one time, I'd even agreed with them. But now? Now I knew that Kiel would have been a loving and protective father. Now I realized what women like me were giving up because some fat old men in Washington didn't think that I, as a single mother, was capable of making that kind of decision for my child.

It was bullshit, but I was literally powerless to change it. At least in the next few days. After that? Well, maybe I'd start a YouTube campaign using some of the things I'd learned on the Colony. Maybe I could get some single mothers to band together and send petitions to congress. Something. There had to be *something*.

"One thing at a time." I was talking to myself, but I had to focus. Wyatt needed me first. I'd worry about the rest later.

Tears burned behind my eyes but I blinked them away with the brutal efficiency of a single mother who was used to making hard choices and hiding tears that wanted to fall. Nothing was easy. Crying about it wasn't going to make it hurt less, it was just going to show the world the chink in my armor, a weakness to exploit. The pain caused by my dead palm, no one else would ever know about. I just knew, some-where in the universe, another palm was just as dark, just as cold and empty.

But Kiel wasn't the only one who wanted me. Wyatt *needed* me. I couldn't afford to be weak. I was a single mother. Losing my shit was simply not an option.

The warden walked me to the front doors of the processing center and waited as the car I'd summoned using a phone app arrived to take me home.

"Thank you," I said.

She tilted her head to the side with a slight nod. "You're welcome. Just be sure you keep our agreement."

"I will." The glass doors slid open and I ran for the car pulling up to the curb. The sun was just starting to set and I glanced again at my phone. Just after eight, which meant Wyatt would going to bed soon and I wanted to see him, needed to feel his sweet little arms wrap around my neck, needed him to smother me with little boy love so the empty hole where Kiel had been wouldn't hurt quite so much. I wanted to heal him immediately, not wait another second to see the pain be taken away.

I missed both my boys right now, and the pain in my heart threatened to break me. The pain of my dead palm? I'd live with it as a constant reminder of Kiel and what we shared.

We pulled away and I looked up at the processing center in time to see the doctor who'd help send me to the Colony watching the car pull away from a second story window. I gasped.

"Shit."

One phone call and the Senator would know I was back. They'd be knocking on my door the moment I got home. Time for Plan B.

I needed to run. I needed to get Wyatt out of that apartment as soon as possible. My fumbling fingers struggled with pulling up my mom's number.

She answered her phone on the first ring.

"Mom."

"Oh my god, Lindsey! You're back! I was so afraid you wouldn't make it." She burst into tears and I heard my little boy yelling and whooping in the background. *Mommy's back! Mommy's back! Mommy's back!*

"Are you packed, like I told you to?" I whispered. While the driver wasn't paying me any attention, I didn't want him to know anything. "Cash and passports for all three of us?"

My mother's voice settled and she ignored Wyatt's chanting. "The just in case, bag?"

"Yes." I'd asked her to be ready to leave town in a hurry, leave and never come back. Just in case. It seemed, just in case time was here.

"Yes, dear. We're ready."

I signed. "Good. Load the bags in the car." I leaned back in the seat, watching the streetlights float by in a blur caused by tears I refused to let fall. "Get in the car right now. Don't wait. They know I'm back. Get in the car and meet me where we talked about. Ditch your cell and use the burner phone I bought for you. If you need me, call me on my new number. I wrote the number in your wallet."

The designated meeting place was a run down, flea-bag motel about twenty miles out of town on an old state highway. I had our route planned out. We'd cut across the wetlands to the gulf and ride the coast until we got to Texas. After that? Well, Mexico was an option. Maybe we'd hop a plane and head farther south. Costa Rica. Hell, Peru. I'd get ahold of Warden Egara and get her the magic wand, but first I had to make sure Wyatt was safe.

"All right, honey. We'll be there as soon as we can."

"Hurry, mom. These guys don't play around."

I hung up and gave the driver new directions. I wasn't one to bite my nails, but I was wound so tight I was pretty sure I wouldn't have a single fingernail left by the time we got to the motel. Heart pounding, I settled back in the seat, pushed the button to lower the window and threw my cell phone out onto a bank of grass so it wouldn't shatter. I hoped they would try to track my cell. Hoped someone would pick it up and start moving, preferably in the opposite direction.

Stop. Go. Drive. Stop. The seconds ticked by like hours and I would swear that damn car hit every red light between me and my baby.

Every single fucking red light. And every time we stopped moving, it felt like the shadows were stalking me. Watching. Waiting.

I breathed a sigh of relief when the driver pulled into the motel parking lot. I tipped him a twenty and asked him to forget he ever saw me, told him I was running from a psycho, abusive ex-boyfriend who beat me. The guy frowned and gave me back the twenty. Said to keep it since I might need it more than him. When he drove away, I was confident he wouldn't talk, at least not for a while.

My old beat up sedan with Wyatt's booster seat in the back was parked outside the fifth blue door. A flash of blond hair disappeared behind a swinging curtain seconds before the door opened. And just like that, I could breathe.

Wyatt's smile could have lit cities as he hurried to me as fast as he could. His pace was slow and awkward, the brace on his leg keeping him from going as quickly as he wanted. I lifted him up and hugged him close as he buried his face in my neck and squeezed as hard as his little arms could squeeze.

God, he smelled so good, felt so soft, warm. Sweet.

"I missed you, Mommy."

Those words. My heart cracked into a thousand pieces. "I missed you, too, baby."

"Don't ever go away again."

I couldn't stop the tears now. They streamed down my face like water from a faucet. "I won't, Wyatt. I promise. Never again."

I carried him into the hotel room where my mom was waiting, gave her a quick hug and settled Wyatt down on one of the hard beds. She looked at me with concerned eyes, although she had the relieved look of a mother who sent her child out into the world for the first time. I hadn't really thought of how brave she was, letting me go into space. God, she'd sent her child into space!

I reached across and squeezed her hand and she gave me a watery smile in return.

"I have something special to show you."

Wyatt clapped his hands like he was about to get a present, so I had to clarify. "You can't keep it, but some very nice people let Mommy borrow it to heal your leg."

My mom stepped closer, her hand coming to rest on my shoulder, eyes wide. "What? What are you talking about?"

I looked up into her confused face and smiled through my tears. "You aren't going to believe this." I reached into my purse and pulled out the ReGen wand. Activating it the way Rachel had taught me, I took off Wyatt's brace and pushed Wyatt's dinosaur pajamas up above his knee, which was foolish, because the healing would all happen below the surface, but I wanted to watch him. I needed to see.

"Don't be afraid," I told him. My heart was beating so hard I was sure Wyatt could hear it. This was it. I could heal my child, make him whole, with just a wave of this wand. No surgery. No pain.

The wand turned blue and Wyatt's eyes rounded. "What is it?" he asked with his perfect little lisp.

I grinned, happier than I'd been since the accident. "A magic wand. I brought it back from outer space just for you."

"Really?" The cowlick on the top of his head had gone a bit wild and cute little spikes of pale blond hair shot straight up off his head like sprouts of grass. "Do you know the magic word?"

"Of course, I do." I leaned down and kissed him on the nose. That done, I lifted the wand over his leg and said, "Abracadabra."

Wyatt's excitement faded and he grew serious, lying back on the bed where my mother quickly moved to prop some pillows behind him. The routine was old and too familiar.

But this would be the last time. Ever.

I held the wand over him, moving it over his leg until the indicator light Rachel taught me to watch blinked at me that the ReGen wand had done its job. I hadn't kept track of time, but it couldn't have been more than a minute, maybe two. That was it. Two minutes and he was healed—I hoped. I ran it over the rest of him then, just to be sure. If there was anything wrong with him, anything I didn't know about, I wanted it fixed. Cured. Healed. I wanted him perfect.

When I was finished, I looked at my son, at the sleepy, contented expression on his face.

"How does that feel, baby?"

Wyatt's little smile brought the tears back. "It doesn't hurt, Mommy."

"Show me."

He looked to me, then my mom, who nodded. He hopped down from the bed, his pajama leg sliding back in place. Yes, he hopped. No tentative step. He looked to me, eyes wide. Then he jumped. Mom put her arms out, instinctively ready to stop him.

"It's all better!" he said, then ran across the room to the bathroom door, then back. "Mommy, it's all better."

My mom put her hand to her mouth, trying to cover her tears. Tears, I knew, were of joy, not sorrow. Her eyes met mine. "All better."

I nodded as Wyatt came back and stood before me.

I ruffled his hair. "All better," I repeated. The relief was incredible. It had worked. No matter what happened in life now, I knew Wyatt was going to be okay.

"That's good, Wyatt. It's time to sleep now."

He climbed in bed easily enough. While I had no doubt he'd want to bounce around the room all night, it was late for him.

"Go to sleep," I said, leaning down and kissing his soft forehead.

"You stay," he insisted.

"I'll stay. I promise."

Wyatt drifted to sleep and my mother and I settled in hard wooden chairs facing one another across a tiny round table. The motel was old, the carpet worn threadbare in front of the door. The overhead light had several flies trapped in the dingy yellow glass and the room smelled like dust, but I didn't care about any of it. Wyatt was healed and we were safely away from the apartment.

My mother leaned forward and crossed her arms over her chest. One eyebrow raised in a look I'd seen hundreds of times. She held out her palm and I gave her the wand.

"Tell me."

She didn't say more. She didn't need to. I had three days to tell her about and ten light years of travel. With Wyatt asleep, I told her everything I dared about the journey, the fighting pits, and about Kiel. The wand. When I was done, I was wiping tears from my eyes and so was she.

"You love him." It wasn't a question.

I shrugged. "How could I? I only knew him for two days."

There went the raised eyebrow again. "You love him."

I wiped the tears from my cheeks and looked at my son. "I love Wyatt."

"But he's your, what? Marked mate?"

I held out my palm so she could see the mark there. The mark that, up until a few days ago, was just a weird birthmark.

"Your father had one like that. And so did his mother. I assumed it was just a weird family trait, like red hair or crooked teeth."

I was stunned by those words. He'd been gone a long time and I didn't remember the little things about him. Especially a mark on his palm. If he had a mark, did that mean my mother was his marked mate?

"You don't have one," I said.

She shook her head.

So my father had once had a marked mate out there somewhere in the universe and never found her? Was she still alive? Did it matter? I knew my parents' marriage had been a happy one. *That* I remembered. That was all my mother knew, perhaps even my father. I hadn't known the mark was a sign I was a descendant of Everis either. I wasn't about to tell my mother her marriage was less because they weren't marked mates.

"Isn't there anything you can do? To be with him...and Wyatt?" she asked, breaking me from my thoughts.

I shook my head sadly. "He doesn't know about Wyatt. I never told him."

"Shame on you, Lindsey." She chastised me and I felt like I was three years old again. "If he loves you, he'll want Wyatt, too. I don't understand why you can't be together."

"Because Earth doesn't allow their volunteers to the Interstellar Brides Program to have children. It's against the rules. You can volunteer to sacrifice your own life and happiness by going to another planet, but I can't make that decision for a minor. It's not allowed."

"Bullshit, Lindsey." My eyes widened. Mom never swore. "You're not a bride. You weren't matched."

"I—" Holy shit. My mom was right.

"If you could take Wyatt and go live on the Colony, would you?"

A sad burst of something close to laughter erupted from my diaphragm. "Yes."

"Why didn't you tell him?"

I couldn't look her in the eye, instead stared at the threadbare carpet. "I don't know. Everything happened so fast and I knew I couldn't stay. It never seemed to be the right time."

The tsking sound made me cringe. "Not every man is like Pet—"

"Don't say his name," I interrupted.

"Fine. Not every man is like the *sperm donor*. You should have told him."

"It's too late, Mom. I'm here and he's all the way across the universe. All that matters is that Wyatt is going to be okay now." I smiled brilliantly knowing he was all better. She turned her head to watch Wyatt as he slept.

"Yes, that is truly a miracle."

She sighed and I really looked at her for the first time since my return. Lines had deepened around her eyes. Her skin was pale. "You're exhausted, Mom. Go to sleep."

It was a testament to her fatigue when she didn't argue, just went to the second bed and pulled back the covers. She kicked off her shoes and climbed in, clothes and all. When her head was settled on the pillow, she looked at me. "When do you want to leave?"

I glanced at the twenty-year-old alarm clock that rested on the bedside table between the two queen sized beds. "Four hours at most."

She nodded and closed her eyes.

I checked the deadbolt and settled onto the bed behind Wyatt. Pulling him into my arms, I buried my nose in his sweet-smelling hair and breathed in little boy and sunshine. Nothing had ever smelled so good.

I was just drifting to sleep when the door burst open, slamming against the stained yellow paper that covered the wall.

All three of us jolted and came awake. My mother cried out and I tugged Wyatt into my arms and tucked him beneath me. I heard his whimpering, but he didn't move.

I looked up into the one face I didn't want to see, Roger, the Senator's henchman. The man who made the deals, offered the money and threatened my son all in one smooth breath. Three days ago I'd been ready to do anything. I'd done it, healed Wyatt in a way I never imagined.

"Roger."

"Ms. Walters. I believe you owe us an explanation."

Behind him, the doctor from the processing center stalked into the room and made a beeline for the ReGen wand lying on the table where my mother and I had left it out. "And I'll be taking this," she said.

"No. You can't."

It was for Warden Egara. We'd made a deal. Wyatt would be healed and she'd get the wand back. I couldn't go back on that, but Roger pulled a gun from some magical place that bad guys always seemed to have weapons hidden and I knew I would have to break my promise.

"We can." He waved the gun between me and my mother, who was sitting up and staring at him wide eyed. Scared. Her eyes kept darting to Wyatt.

"Let my mother and Wyatt go. They have nothing to do with this."

Roger just arched one sinister brow and said, "Get your bags, ladies. You're all coming with us."

I tensed to move, to rise from the bed and try to protect Wyatt, but as I gathered myself a miracle happened...my mark flared with welcome heat and I started to cry.

Wyatt looked from Roger to me, his eyes round and scared. "Don't cry, Mommy."

I smiled at him. "Don't worry. Everything's all right." I turned my head to Roger and saw the confusion in his eyes as my entire demeanor changed and I stood tall and proud before him, absolutely fearless. "If I were you, I'd put the gun down."

"And why is that?" Roger asked.

My grin was genuine, the heat in my palm flaring again. "So my mate doesn't kill you."

CHAPTER 10

iel

"THESE EARTH VEHICLES ARE PATHETIC. I can run faster than this."

Warden Egara ignored me, her eyes on the road, her grip steady on the vehicle's odd driving wheel. "Yes, but for how long?"

She swerved violently around a large vehicle pulling giant boxes on wheels and I grasped the small handle above the window so I would not tumble into her lap. "Several miles."

"Umm, hmm." She straightened out and dashed back into the lane in front of the much larger vehicle. "She could be ten miles away, or a hundred. You wouldn't last that long."

Perhaps not, which was why I'd agreed to fold my body into this cramped seat in this small contraption she called a car. I smelled blood, old blood, but the scent was familiar. "There is blood in this vehicle, but it does not belong to my mate."

She shook her head. "Which way?"

I closed my eyes for a moment and pointed to the bend in the road that took us to the left. She went where I pointed and I drew the scent of the blood deeper into my senses.

"The blood is familiar." My Hunter senses refused to let the matter pass.

"That was months ago, and I cleaned it with bleach twice."

"I recommend you clean it again if you wish to erase all traces. The scent remains."

The warden grinned. "You really are a Hunter, aren't you?"

"Of course." We passed a small side road and I pointed again. "Turn. Now."

She slammed on the brakes and I braced my arms on the small dash as two of the wheels left the ground and the other two squealed. When the car landed safely, she finally answered my question.

"That blood belongs to Jessica. She was injured by a Hive Scout team right before Nial found her."

"The Prime's mate?"

"Yes."

"The Hive Scout team was here? On Earth?"

"Yes."

"Drive faster. We are close." I could feel Lindsey now, practically taste her skin, hear her heart beating. The link between us flared back to life and my palm ignited with welcome heat, a raging inferno of pulsing fire that made my entire body sing with need. My mate was close, and upset. Afraid. As I drew nearer, my instincts reached for her, for the mental connection that came in dream sharing.

I didn't know what was going on, but I knew she was afraid.

Warden Egara came to a stop at a four direction intersection and looked at me. "Which way?"

Lindsey was so close now that her presence drowned out everything but the need to get to her.

I opened the car door and hit the ground running, my speed making me a blur. There was a building ahead with a row of closed doors. Cars were parked in front of each door and I knew my mate was here, somewhere.

I stopped in the center of the parking area and closed my eyes, listening for her heartbeat, her voice.

"Don't cry, Mommy." My heart skipped a beat as I heard the voice of my son for the first time.

"Don't worry. Everything's all right." Lindsey, my brave mate. She was scared, I could hear the wobble in her voice, but she was trying to reassure him.

Her next words chilled me to the bone.

"If I were you, I'd put the gun down."

"And why is that?" The man's voice was deep and calm. Arrogant.

He would die.

"So my mate doesn't kill you."

Lindsey tried to save him, but it was too late. He'd threatened my mate and my son. I had no idea what this place was, but it was not her home. That I knew for certain as others rustled and moved in the spaces behind the adjoining doors.

Silent as a shadow I moved to the door and listened.

Five heartbeats. Five different breathing patterns. The boy's racing pulse was almost birdlike. I could distinguish the sound of four smaller bodies, smell the sweet scents of three females, one of them my mate.

But the other? Metal and male aggression. Battle had a scent, and this man was drenched in the desire to hurt, intimidate, perhaps even kill.

I waited, listening as he ordered them to gather their belongings and go to the door.

A woman I did not recognize came out of the room first.

She was young, similar in age to my Lindsey, her hair was a dark, vibrant red, her clothing similar to what Warden Egara wore, but green.

The doctor who'd betrayed the program. This must be her. She'd been the one to implant Lindsey with the NPU and sneak her into the transport room.

I remained silent and still, waiting in the dark space where light from the closest two lamps failed to reach.

An older woman exited next, and from her looks and the way she moved I knew this was Lindsey's mother.

My mate appeared in the doorway, the coward behind her had moved in front of the glass window.

The moment she passed through the threshold with Wyatt and I knew a stray shot from the man's weapon wouldn't strike her, I leapt.

Glass shattered in an explosion as I lifted my armored elbows up to protect my face and propelled myself through the barrier to leap on the man who'd dared threaten my mate.

His neck cracked in my hands half a second later, the sound one I wished to hear a thousand times over. He slumped to the ground, the weapon he'd used to threaten the woman I loved dropped to the floor with a soft thud. Broken shards of glass slipped from my armor like water from stone and fell to the floor with hundreds of small tinkling sounds I doubted anyone but I could hear.

I tossed the dead man's body aside like trash, forgotten as I turned to my mate.

"Lindsey. Are you unhurt?"

She stood still, shocked for a heartbeat of time that was an agony for me. I needed her, needed to touch her, kiss her, feel her alive and well in my arms.

When I was about to go mad, the spell broke and she cried out, leaping at me, trusting me to catch her.

Her arms were around me, her lips on mine, crushing me with a desperation I felt keenly.

"Kiel!" She tore her lips from mine and I settled her on her feet, my arms around her waist, unwilling to let her go.

"Did he hurt you?"

She shook her head and the tight coil within me began to unwind.

A small hand tugged on my arm and I looked down into a pair of wide blue eyes the same shape as his mother's. "Hey. Who are you?"

Holding onto Lindsey with one hand, I bent down and lifted Wyatt up with the other, holding them both to me as I looked into the eyes of my son and told him the truth. "I am your father now, Wyatt. I love your mommy and I'm going to take care of both of you from now on."

The boy looked at me, then his mother who was crying and clinging to me like I was her world, her everything, as I would be.

"Mommy?"

"What baby?"

"Is he my new daddy?"

Lindsey's smile was so full of love when she looked at her son I felt tears gather in my eyes. By the gods, what I wouldn't give to see her look at me like that, with complete and total unconditional love. "Yes. Is that okay?"

The small man looked at me, raised his hands to my face and turned my head from side to side, exploring, watching, testing me. I noticed the mark of an Everian on his palm, knew he would one day grow strong, perhaps become a Hunter. He looked deeply into my eyes and I saw a soul much older than his young body, knew he had suffered just as his mother had.

I vowed he would suffer no more.

I waited. This moment, how he would react to me, feel

about me, was Wyatt's choice. But he would come with me no matter what. He was part of Lindsey and I loved him already, his courage, his obvious love for his mother. But I would not force this. I would give him all the time he needed to trust me.

Wyatt looked into my eyes. "Will you teach me how to protect mommy so no more bad guys will come?"

His question made my blood boil, and Lindsey gasp, but I gave him my most solemn vow. "Yes, Wyatt. I will teach you how to be a warrior and protect the people you love."

Wyatt nodded slowly, deliberately before laying his sweet head on my shoulder to look at his mother. "Okay. I want to call you Daddy."

Lindsey's shoulders shook and I looked up to see Lindsey's mother watching from the doorway. Tears streaked down her face and I nodded to her in respect and gratitude for giving my mate to me. "Mother."

"Welcome to the family, Kiel." She wiped at her cheeks and lifted her eyes to me. "I hope you know, wherever you take my daughter, I'll be going, too."

I recognized that determined glint in her eye, it was a look I'd seen more than once on Lindsey's face. "Of course."

"All right then." She turned to the parking lot as we both heard a woman's yell. Carrying my mate and son to the doorway so I could see, I found Warden Egara in the parking lot with a weapon pointed at the other female who'd exited the room. She had the gun pressed to the woman's side and was taking the ReGen wand from her outstretched hand.

"I'll take that, Doctor Graves."

"I'm sorry, Katherine." The red haired woman's shoulders slumped in defeat as the warden waved her toward the car, fury evident in her gaze.

"Save it for your lawyer."

* * *

Kiel, Personal Quarters, The Colony

IT WAS ONLY when I had Lindsey in my quarters, the almost silent *whoosh* of the door closing behind us that I breathed again. Every tense line of my body eased. My mark was warm and alive once more. My heart didn't ache.

"Kiel," she said. Just my name, nothing more, but I heard the worry in her tone.

Fuck. I didn't want her to worry ever again.

I'd held her hand ever since we left that hovel of doors where I'd found her. I didn't plan to stop touching her anytime soon. I'd held Wyatt securely in one arm, my other slung around Lindsey's shoulders as we transported. Lindsey's mom, Carla, held her daughter's hand, surprisingly calm since she had never transported before and was leaving her planet behind for good. Both of them had been fitted with new NPU's, courtesy of Warden Egara, who'd given us both a tight hug and told us to get the hell off the planet before anything else went wrong.

But now we were home, I tugged Lindsey into me, wrapping my arms about her and just reveling in her being her. With me.

"Are you sure they're okay?" she asked, her words muffled by my shirt.

I was eager to be with Wyatt, too. To learn about him, see his smiles, watch as his eyes widened at discovering the world—no, the universe—around him. But we had the rest of our lives for that. Tomorrow would be soon enough. Tonight, tonight I had to claim my marked mate, make her mine. I couldn't wait any longer, and while she didn't understand it as I did, neither could she.

She hadn't grown up with the knowledge of what this claiming meant. Being so far apart had been agony, but having her so close, yet unclaimed, was another kind of torture. My body ached for hers, as I was sure hers did for mine. Only when we were truly claimed would our bodies, our minds, our hearts, finally be soothed.

I wanted to claim Lindsey, my mate, but I had to soothe Lindsey, the mother, first.

"You saw Rachel, she is beside herself with having a little boy here. Your mother is with Wyatt so he has a familiar face, but he is eager to see where you traveled. Rachel and her mates will give them a tour. I have no doubt that he will run around as any little boy should and be ready to sleep soon. I am not familiar with the impact of transport on one so small, but Rachel will monitor him closely."

I saw her glance toward the door. I recognized her worried look.

I tapped the comm unit on my wrist. "Governor Rone."

"Kiel. I expected to have no communication from you this evening now that your mate is with you again."

Yes, talking to Maxim was not my top priority. But I could not fuck Lindsey as I wished, to claim her as we both needed, if her mind was elsewhere. I wanted her focused solely on me sinking into her so deep we didn't know where one ended and the other began.

"How is Wyatt?" I asked, not responding to his comment.

Neither of us could miss the sound of a little boy squealing in delight. "Again!" the small voice said.

"Ryston is carrying him through the air as if he were a Prillon battle cruiser."

Yes, the boy was just fine and I felt Lindsey relax within my hold.

"Do not concern yourself with our newest members of

Base 3. Both are content. Rachel has arranged their guest quarters for tonight."

"Is that a phone? Is Lindsey there?" Lindsey's mom's voice interrupted the governor and I couldn't help but smile at that breach in protocol. When I heard the stoic man laugh, I was relieved to know he was enjoying himself as well.

"I'm here, Mom," Lindsey said. She'd learned in her few days here how the comm units worked. Her mother and Wyatt adapting even more quickly as Doctor Sornen made sure to keep them comfortable during the inevitable headache. Now Wyatt loved to run around and chat with every warrior on base. Even more astonishing, the more Hive technology they displayed, the more he wanted to investigate and talk to them.

Never in a thousand years would I expect Hive contaminated warriors to show-off their implants. But the man with the most silver always won Wyatt's undivided attention, as I was more than ready to give mine to the beautiful woman in my arms.

"Honey, you enjoy your time with Kiel. Wyatt and I are just fine. We'll see you tomorrow. Or the day after."

"Again!" Wyatt shouted in the background.

"Satisfied?" I whispered.

Lindsey looked up at me and nodded. "Tomorrow," I said, then broke the connection.

"I know you will want to see Wyatt in the morning. We will move to a different space so there is a bedroom for Wyatt beside ours. As for your mother, I am sure she will be content with her own space nearby."

I liked Lindsey's mother, based on the brief time I'd known her, and she was brave and kind. It was obvious where my mate got her fair hair and beautiful eyes. While she was older than most warriors on The Colony, there were some here of comparable age and I imagined one would capture her heart soon enough.

"You see, they are well occupied." I kissed the top of Lindsey's head, her silky hair soft against my lips. "As for you, I have plans to keep you well occupied as well."

She tilted her head back to look up at me, her blue eyes filled with love—and heat. "You do?"

"Mmm, my brave mate. It seems we have both traveled across the universe for each other."

"I'd do it again, too."

My heart softened at those words. Yes, I was a hardened warrior, a Hunter, yet I would bend and yield to only her. "As would I." I gave her a fierce squeeze, then pushed her away. "Yet we will have no reason to do so. It was as if my arm had been ripped off."

She nodded, licked her lips. "Yes."

"I wish to claim you, Lindsey from Earth."

A brilliant smile spread across her face. "Lindsey from The Colony," she countered. The governor had approved her transfer and arrival and granted her immediate citizenship. As she was not an official bride, she did not need to abide by their customs. Wyatt I'd taken as my son and transported him away from Earth without permission. Thankfully, Maxim had not bothered to argue. Neither had anyone on Earth. Seemed a small boy could disappear and no one noticed. Which was fine by me. He was mine now. As was his mother.

"I do not know the custom behind your Earth bonding ceremony, but I want to claim you, make you mine. Permanently. Irrevocably. I can't do it without your consent."

"Yes," she breathed.

I lifted her hand to my mouth, turned it so I kissed her palm. Her mark. I felt the heat of it against my lips. "Be mine."

"And will you be mine?" she asked, a coy lilt to her words.

"Yes, body and soul. I just need to get you naked, get inside that hot, wet pussy and fill you with my seed."

"Then I'll be yours?" she asked.

"Then you'll be claimed," I clarified. "But only if I do all that while our marks touch."

She took my hand, the mirror to hers and curled her fingers around mine so our palms touched. "Like this?"

I nodded and started to walk forward, forcing her to back up, step by step, toward our bed. "Yes, but we will have to let go if we are to get naked."

She opened her hand and stepped back. Her hands moved to her top and I shook my head. "Remember, mate. That's my job."

This was it, the time to claim my mate. Make this beautiful Earth female mine forever.

* * *

Lindsey

THIS WAS IT. He was going to claim me and then nothing could separate us. Never again. I was glad Kiel wanted to take off my clothes for me. My hands were shaking, I was so eager for him. He'd said we'd be hot for each other, the need to fuck getting stronger and stronger until he claimed me. He hadn't been lying. Of course, I'd been heartbroken and distracted going back to Earth, but now? Now I wanted him with a ferocity, a need I never imagined. I was so wet, he could push me back onto the bed and take me right now.

I wasn't going to last. Whenever he touched me, my nipples, my pussy, I was going to go off like a whole Fourth of July fireworks display.

He wasn't patient this time. My clothes were strewn across the floor within seconds and I was picked up and tossed onto the bed.

My mate had come across the universe to save me and bring me home. I loved this caveman behavior. God, it turned me on.

Well, everything about him turned me on. His voice, his scent, every inch of his body he was quickly exposing as he stripped off his clothes. His gorgeous cock—and the way it filled me up.

As soon as the birth control shot wore off, there was no doubt I'd get pregnant right away. He was so virile, just looking at him made my ovaries perk up. I wanted a baby with him. A little girl that had his dark hair. A little girl that would wrap Kiel around her little finger. And Wyatt would be taught to watch out for her by his father, the protector — my Kiel.

When he was bare before me, I reached a hand out to him, bent my knees and put my feet on the bed so I was open to him.

I heard the growl as he came over me.

"Mate, you tempt me so," he said. His dark eyes met mine. "I'm too out of control. This claiming, it will be fast. But then we will have all night."

That was what he'd said the first time he took me. Had it been a few short days ago? He'd been eager then, coming quickly, but that had allowed him to take me all night long. And wow, he had endurance. I'd been eager for him then, knowing our time had been short, that I was leaving. Now, I shook my head, my hair brushing across the bed. "We'll have forever."

He grinned then. "Forever," he repeated.

With one hand on my knee, he spread me wider for him. Just as I'd thought, I was so wet the head of his cock slid over my pussy, settled against my opening and slid into me in one long, forceful stroke.

He groaned, I screamed. I came, just like that.

My inner walls clenched around him, milking him, pulling him deeper.

His hand found mine and our fingers intertwined. I looked up at him, watched him watch me.

"You're too perfect. Too good. It feels so fucking good. I claim you, Lindsey. My mate. My love. My heart."

Each word was punctuated by a deep thrust. I angled my hips to take him deeper, loving the after effects of my orgasm. I watched as his need took over, his eyes narrowing, his hips speeding up, losing the even tempo.

"Mine," he said, then repeated again and again. He shouted it, the one word bouncing off the walls of the room as he stiffened above me, buried deep. I felt the heat of him, his very essence, spill into me. Fill me, coat me. Mark me.

Claim me.

"Mine," I repeated.

When Kiel caught his breath, he didn't pull out, didn't flop down on the bed beside me. No, he stayed hard and deep inside me.

"Again."

"Now?" I asked, surprised.

His hand squeezed mine where our marks touched.

"All night, mate. All night."

Oh god.

He began to move then, took me hard and fast, sweet and slow, in every position, in every way.

All. Night. Long.

EPILOGUE

L̲indsey, The Colony, Four Months Later...

"I swear this baby is going to come out fully grown." Rachel waddled over to a chair and lowered herself down beside me with uncharacteristic lack of grace. "I can't believe I have three more months to go."

"At least you aren't on bed rest like Kristin." I couldn't help but smile. She might be grouchy because she was as big as a house, but her baby was precious, a beacon of hope for the entire planet. As with Kristin's impending delivery, everyone was anxious. While Wyatt was the first child, Kristin and Rachel would be the first brides to give birth on the planet and the first babies born from mates brought together by the Interstellar Brides Program. All the warriors were as anxious and eager as their mates.

Kristin, Hunt and Tyran were nowhere to be seen. Probably hiding away in their private quarters peeling her grapes and hand feeding her between orgasms.

Lucky woman.

Maxim and Ryston watched Rachel closely. Ryston took a step in our direction, but Rachel waved him off. He didn't look pleased to be dismissed and kept watch from afar.

"Well, your mates are big," I replied. "Makes sense the baby would be big, too."

"Yeah, well, it would help if the little peanut wasn't punching my insides like a prize fighter." Rachel grimaced and waved her mates away, clearly annoyed by their hovering.

Laughing, I glanced across the open expanse behind the main Base 3 building. A flat area covered with benches and trees, flowers from all over the universe and soft, springy grass, the park was the place of outdoor amusement now. We were watching Wyatt run circles around several of the warriors. After all these months, a routine had been created and many of the warriors on the Colony arrived promptly after lunch for afternoon playtime. Playtime—the term was ours—Rachel, Kristin and I had called Wyatt's daily routine that based on Earth custom—but I wasn't sure who the *play time* was for. No one could tell who was enjoying it more, Wyatt or the fully grown Atlans, Prillons, Vikens and other warriors he treated like his personal jungle gym.

A huge Atlan was shifting back and forth from beast mode and chasing Wyatt, making him scream and giggle so hard his face had turned pink. That sound brought both a thrill and love to my heart. Kiel stepped out of the group of men who were playing some game with a ball, similar to football, but had rules I still didn't understand. Kiel grabbed Wyatt and tossed him up in the air. The boy squealed in delight. "Again, Daddy!"

I bit my lip, trying not to let emotion swamp me. Wyatt had started to call Kiel *Daddy* right from the start. To say that my mate considered my little boy to be his was obvious. He was protective, watchful, caring and had done so much to teach him Hunter ways already. The little mark on Wyatt's palm indicated he had the genes to follow in Kiel's footsteps. Someday. For now, I was content with him being carried on everyone's shoulders. He had to grow up a bit before he could start hunting for bad guys.

Rachel had been watching the group of warriors play as well and she rubbed her swollen belly with a smile on her face. "I think he's going to come out Wyatt-sized," Rachel added.

I reached over and patted her hand. "It could be a girl. *She* could be Wyatt sixed."

Rachel choked on her laugh. "Please, don't even say it."

"Your mates are going to be in serious trouble with a baby girl," my mother said. She was seated on the other side of me, but she'd leaned forward to look at Rachel. Beside her was Ryston's mother, who'd moved to The Colony from Prillon a few months before our arrival. Being of similar age, the two older women had hit it off from the start and were very close friends, even though they were from two different planets.

"Yes, a girl would change everything around here," Ryston's mother said. "All these males need more females about, even if one's just a baby."

Rachel rolled her eyes. "Poor little thing. She'd scrape her knee and my mates would lose their minds."

My mother laughed and I noticed a couple heads turn in our direction. My mom was in her mid-forties and, since our arrival here, had blossomed. No stress. A new friend. She looked ten years younger and glowed with happiness. I had a feeling it wouldn't be long before a few of the warriors began to express interest. Ryston's mother was Prillon, and I didn't know her as well, but she walked with a regal bearing that, as of yet, none of the warriors had dared approach. But with her mates both gone now, her grieving would only protect her for so long. She was not too old to start again. Both of the women might be beyond the age to bear children, but there were plenty of older warriors around who would be happy simply to have their affection and company.

"With the three new mates that are now on Base 5, I have a feeling there will be many babies on all the Colony bases soon enough," I said with some pride. The videos I'd given Warden Egara had begun to work. More Earth women were signing up for the program and requesting to be sent to the Colony. Every woman who arrived was a blessing and a gift to the rest of the warriors. First Base 3, with the arrival of Rachel. Now Base 5. Soon the other bases would see their first brides as well.

"You've done good work with Warden Egara," my mother said. "I heard a single mother with a ten-year old girl just transported to Base 5."

"What?" I hadn't heard that, but I wasn't surprised. The warden was eager to see the warriors here matched, especially now that my stories of life on The Colony were being published—through the Interstellar Brides Program marketing. I sent the warden a new warrior profile and interview every week. The PR for the Colony was better than it had ever been. And the warden had petitioned Earth's governments to allow single mothers to volunteer. "I want to meet them."

"Base 5 is on the other side of the planet," Ryston's mother reminded me. That *was* rather far away. But still... they invented transporters for a reason, right?

"This baby's at least the size of Wyatt, if not a ten-year old," Rachel grumbled, her hand rubbing over her big belly. "I don't care if it's a girl or a boy. At this point, I just want it out."

I laughed, as did the two older mothers around us, the sound of it carrying to the warriors. Rachel's gasp of pain was barely more than a whisper as she pressed down on her stomach, hard, just beneath her ribs.

Maxim and Ryston turned, dark looks on their faces and dashed over to Rachel. "You are well?"

Rachel rolled her eyes. "Mates, I am fine. Your baby likes to play footsies with my ribs."

"Water?"

"A pillow?"

The mates began listing everything they could possibly get for Rachel. "Boys. Enough. I promise to tell you when it's time by saying, *'It's time.'*"

Neither mate liked that answer based on their narrowed eyes, the way Maxim crossed his arms over his chest. Ryston leaned down, scooped up Rachel into his arms as if she were light as a feather and not carrying a watermelon-sized baby.

"Boys? You didn't call us *boys* last night," her mate growled, stalking off toward the entrance to the living quarters. "I believe you referred to me as a god. We will remind you."

"Ladies," Maxim bowed to the three of us, gave us a wink, then followed his family. With his quick pace, I judged him to be just as impatient to seduce his mate as his second.

"These warriors are a lusty bunch," my mother said. I couldn't help but feel the blush heat my cheeks. I wasn't getting into this conversation with her, especially since my mate was one of the warriors she was speaking of, and he was definitely lusty.

My birth control shot had worn off and we were hoping for a baby of our own. Kiel was very attentive to this task, last night especially. Perhaps that was why I was so tired today. Instead of joining in on the fun, I was content sitting and watching.

Kiel came over then, dangling Wyatt upside down by his

ankles. He carefully dropped him into his grandmother's lap. "You're all sweaty," she told him.

"I was Hunting," he told her. "An Atlan beast."

"Did you catch him?" grandma asked, tickling his belly.

"Of course he did. Wyatt is an exceptional Hunter."

My son glowed at Kiel's praise and something scared and needy settled in me. I'd been so afraid for my son before, raising him alone, trying to be his everything. I would have done the best I could, but every day I worried that I wasn't going to be enough. That I'd fail.

Now we had Kiel. I had a mate who adored both me and our son. And Wyatt was his now. I saw my mate's love for Wyatt in his eyes, in the patience he showed, the way he got down on one knee and looked Wyatt in the eye when he spoke to our son, as if the small boy was the center of his world. As if Wyatt really *mattered*.

Wyatt's small chin jutted out in a stubborn look he'd already adopted from his new father and I hid a grin behind my hand. "When I grow up, I'm going to be the best Hunter ever. Right, Daddy?"

"Yes. The very best."

They began talking then, but I tuned them out, for I only had eyes for Kiel. He stepped close, leaned down so his hands were on the armrests of my outdoor chair. "Hello, mate."

"Hello," I whispered back.

"I think the governor and his second have the right idea."

I arched a brow. "Oh?"

"A little inside play time."

My nipples tightened at the timbre of his voice.

I flicked a gaze to Wyatt.

"Your mother wants more grandchildren," he said to me. My mother grinned, but kept her head facing her grandson until Kiel raised his voice. "Isn't that right?"

"At least three," my mother replied without looking. She

might have been chatting with Wyatt, but she'd definitely been eavesdropping.

"You'll keep Wyatt while I see to that?" he asked my mother. His eyes held mine and he was grinning now.

My face must have been as red as a tomato. "Kiel," I muttered.

"Of course. Take your time. Do things right. Maybe go for twins."

"Mother!" The word was half laugh, half squeal as Kiel scooped me up, just as Ryston had Rachel.

"Playtime for Mommy and Daddy!" Kiel told Wyatt, who nodded his head enthusiastically.

"I want a brudder," Wyatt announced.

"Oh my god," I said, punching ineffectively at Kiel's chest as he walked me into the building, cradled in his arms. "Everyone will know."

I felt him shrug. "So? If they want a mate, they can get one of their own. You're mine." Those two words were a growl that went right to my clit.

I relaxed in his arms and lifted my hands to his chin so he'd look down at me.

"I love you, you know."

"I love you, too, my beautiful mate."

FIND YOUR MATCH!

YOUR mate is out there. Take the test today and discover your perfect match. Are you ready for a sexy alien mate (or two)?

VOLUNTEER NOW!
interstellarbridesprogram.com

WANT MORE?

Sign up for Grace's VIP Reader list at
http://freescifiromance.com

Read the first chapter of HER CYBORG BEAST!

CJ, Interstellar Bride Processing Center, Earth

"I stand. No bed." A deep, rumbling voice filled my head. My mind. My body. This body knew that voice. Knew it and shivered in anticipation. Somehow I knew this male was mine. He was huge. Not in his normal state. He had some kind of sickness. A fever that would cause him to go insane if I didn't tame him. Fuck him. Make him mine forever.

I felt the softness of a bed at my back—my *naked* back—and then I was hoisted up as if I weighed nothing. That was a joke because I weighed plenty. I wasn't a tiny waif or a Victoria's Secret model. Well, I was tall like one, just over six feet, but I had boobs and hips. Strong hands banded about my waist, spun me about so my back was pressed to his front. His *naked* front. Hands slid up and cupped my breasts.

Oh.

Wow.

Um.

Yes. God, yes.

This was crazy. Completely crazy. I didn't like to be manhandled. Hell, I did the manhandling. I ate weak men for breakfast and made stronger ones cry by lunchtime. All in a day's work.

But I wasn't at work now.

I had no idea where the hell I was, but this guy knew just how to push every one of my hot buttons. Or should I say, *her* hot buttons. I wasn't me. Well, I was here, but this wasn't me. The thoughts going through my head, the knowledge, wasn't mine. But the reactions? One tug on my nipples and my pussy was wet and aching. Empty.

I felt the hot throb of his cock against my back. He was tall, really tall based on how far down the bed was from me now. Yet his hands cupped all of my breasts. They usually were overflowing. Triple Ds tended to do that, but not with him. Nope.

I felt...small.

But, this wasn't me. Was it?

It *felt* like me.

"Better," he growled, walking us both slowly toward a table. We were in some kind of room, sterile and impersonal, like a hotel room with a big bed, table and chairs. I couldn't see much else, but I wasn't looking because as soon as my thighs bumped into the cool edge of the table, he leaned forward, forcing me down over the top. I resisted. "Down, mate."

Mate?

I bristled at the firm hand pushing me down, at his commanding tone. That word. I wasn't anyone's mate. I didn't date. I fucked, sure, but I was the one to walk away. I was the one on top, in control. But now? I had zero control, and it was uncomfortable. But the need to let go, to let this guy take over? I wanted it. Well, my pussy did. My nipples did, too. And the woman whose body I inhabited, she wanted it, too. But unlike me, she wasn't afraid. She didn't fight this, or him.

She resisted because she knew he wanted her to. Knew it would make his cock hard and his pulse race. Knew it would push him to the edge of control. She wanted to make sure that when it came to control, she had none. The thought of the cuffs—cuffs?—she knew were coming made her pussy clench with heat.

Which was just damn weird to me, but there was nothing I could do about it. I was a witness and participant, but I wasn't really here. I felt like a ghost inside her body, living someone else's fantasy.

Hot fantasy, sure. But not real. This wasn't real.

This body was all about letting the big brute do anything he wanted. My mind had other ideas. But I had no control here. This body wasn't mine. The thoughts going through my head weren't mine either. This woman—me—whoever I was right now—wanted to push him. She wanted to be dominated. She wanted to be conquered. Controlled. Fucked until she screamed. And I was simply along for the ride. "I don't like to be bossed around," she/I said.

"Liar." I saw a big hand settle onto the table beside me, saw the blunt fingers, the scars, the dusting of hair on the wrist. Felt the other big hand pressing into my back. Harder. More insistent.

I hissed when my breasts came in contact with the hard surface, and I put my elbows out to keep from being lowered all the way, but he changed tactics, his hand moving from my back to my pussy, two fingers sliding deep. "Wet. Mine."

I felt the broad expanse of his torso against my back, his

skin hot, the hard length of his cock rubbing along my wet slit, teasing. And he was right. I was wet. Hot. So eager for him I was afraid this crazy woman—whose body I currently inhabited—was going to break down and *beg. Beg!*

His lips brushed along my spine, fingers slid my hair to the side, and his kisses continued along my neck as his hands worked their magic. One pressing me slowly, inevitably toward a prone position on the table. The other rubbed my bare bottom, huge fingers dipping toward my core, sliding deep, retreating to stroke my sensitive bottom again in a repetitive tease that made me squirm.

The gesture was gentle, reverent even, and completely at odds with his dominance. Two metal bracelets came into my view as he set them down in front of me. Silver toned, they were thick and wide, with decorative etchings in them.

The sight made me hotter, the woman's reaction nearly orgasmic. She wanted them on her wrists, heavy and permanent. They would mark her as his mate. Forever.

I had no idea where they came from, but my mind wasn't working properly, and I couldn't figure it out. Not with the soft lips, the flick of his tongue, the prodding of his cock over my slick folds and the rush of longing filling me.

The bracelets looked old and matched ones that were already on his wrists. I hadn't noticed them before now, but that didn't surprise me.

He shifted, opening one and putting it on my wrist, then the other. Even though I was pressed into the table by his formidable body, I didn't feel threatened. It felt like he was giving me a gift of some kind, something precious.

I just had no idea what.

"They're beautiful," I heard myself say.

He growled again, the rumbling of it vibrating from his chest and into my back. "Mine. Bad girl. Fuck now."

I had no idea why I'd be a bad girl, especially if his cock was as big as it felt. I wanted it.

"Yes. Do it!" I spread my legs wider, not sure what he expected, but knowing I didn't care. I wanted him to fuck me now. I didn't want to be good. I wanted to be bad. Very, very bad.

Evidently, I'd lost my mind because I had no idea what he looked like. Who he was. Where I was. But none of that mattered. And why did the idea of being manhandled or even spanked appeal like it never had before?

He shifted his hips, slid his cock over my folds, and it settled at my entrance. I felt the broad head, so big that it parted my slick lips, and as he pressed in, I whimpered.

He was huge. Like enormous. He was careful as he filled me, as if he knew he might be too much.

I shifted my hips, tried to take him, but my inner walls clenched and squeezed, tried to adjust. My hands couldn't find purchase on the smooth surface, and I lowered myself down, put my cheek against the wood, angling my hips up.

He slid in a touch farther.

I gasped, shook my head. "Too big." My voice was soft, breathy. He wasn't. He'd fit. He might hurt me, might shock me, but I wanted him. Every damn inch.

"Shh," he crooned.

From nowhere, a memory surfaced of this male speaking to me when I'd been worried about this moment. His beast— what was a beast?—*You can take a beast's cock. You were made for it. You were made for me.*

As he slid in to the hilt and I felt his hips press against my bottom, I had to agree with him. I was milking him and clenching down, adjusting to being filled so much, but it felt good.

God, did it ever.

"Ready, mate?"

Ready? For what? He was already in.

But when he pulled back all the way so my folds clung to him before he plunged deep, I realized I hadn't been ready.

The pounding stole the breath from my lungs, but I almost came. I had no idea how because I'd never come from just vaginal penetration only. I needed to rub my clit with my own fingers.

When he did it again, I realized fingers were definitely not needed.

"Yes!" I cried. I couldn't help it. I wanted it. Needed it. I shimmied, pressed back as he plunged in once more.

His hand moved, gripped my wrists, held onto the bracelets.

He held me down and fucked me.

There was no escape. No reprieve. No stopping him as the orgasm built into a dangerous thing. And I wanted all of it. I wanted *him*.

"Come. Now. Scream. I fill you up."

He was a dirty talker, too. Not much for complete sentences, but that was part of his charm.

I was so drenched for him I could hear the wet slap of our bodies as he pounded into me. I could feel the wet coating in the cool air, slipping from me and down my thighs.

Holding me down with one hand, he grabbed my bottom with the other, a full lobe in his grasp, pulling me open. Wider.

He pushed deeper. Harder. I thrashed on the table, both excited and vulnerable, stretched out before him. Unable to move. Unable to resist. I had to accept whatever he wanted to give me. Trust. Surrender.

The thought made me groan, my body spiraling ever higher as I fought, holding back my final fall.

He released my bottom, a single sharp spank landing like liquid heat on my bare skin. And that orgasm he commanded from me? The one I was holding back? Yeah, there it was. I screamed, arched my back, my hard nipples chafing against the table top as I lost control, went blind, an abyss opening up to swallow me as I shattered.

I lost all sense of myself, my only reality the hard thrust of his cock as he pumped into me as my pussy milked him.

"Mate," he said, just before he sank deep, settled, then roared like an animal.

It was like a beast had filled him, taken over. Claimed me.

I felt his seed, hot and thick, coating me deep inside. It was too much for me to hold as he moved again, fucking me through his release, his hot seed sliding from me and down my thighs.

I felt so good and so wrong. Controlled. Overpowered. Blatantly claimed.

Bad. Bad. Bad. I was soooo bad right now.

I didn't even try to get up, not even when he released my wrists and grabbed my hips to pull me back. Hard. He lifted my ass off the table and pulled me onto his cock which was already swelling. Ready for more.

I groaned, trying to move my arms. No luck, but something rattled. The sound odd. Out of place.

"Stay." He grunted the order and thrust into me again. Submitting to him went against everything I was, and yet... my pussy clenched with his barked command. Perhaps I wasn't everything I imagined.

His fingers dug deep, pulling me back until he bottomed out inside me.

Yes!

I was hot all over again. Ready for more. Needy. I could go for hours...

"Caroline." The voice came from out of nowhere. Cold. Clinical. A woman's voice.

Who?

Everything faded even as I struggled to stay in that body, as he pulled out and slowly filled me again. Spread me open. I groaned, fighting for it. Fighting to stay with him.

"Caroline!" Sharp this time. Insistent. Like a teacher scolding her student.

Oh God. The testing...

I gasped—this time not from pleasure—and my eyes flew open.

Instead of bracelets about my wrists, I had restraints. I was naked, but I wasn't bent over with my lover's hands on my hips. I was shackled to a medical exam chair wearing an Interstellar Brides Processing Center gown. The logo tracked up and down the hospital-style gown in neat, perfect rows of burgundy on gray fabric.

Clinical. Sterile. All business.

I wasn't pressed over a hard table. I wasn't being filled and fucked until my entire body exploded. There was no giant man.

There was only me and a stern looking woman in her late twenties. Gray eyes. Dark brown hair coiled tightly into a bun at the base of her skull. She looked like a grumpy ballerina, and her name floated to the surface even before I read her name tag.

Warden Egara. She was doing my testing. Testing for the Interstellar Brides Program. A process which would match me to an alien and send me into outer space to be his wife.

Forever.

Read more now!

CONNECT WITH GRACE

Interested in joining my not-so-secret Facebook Sci-Fi Squad? Get excerpts, cover reveals and sneak peeks before anyone else. Be part of a closed Facebook group that shares pictures and fun news. JOIN Here: http://bit.ly/SciFiSquad

All of Grace's books can be read as sexy, stand-alone adventures. Her Happily-Ever-Afters are always free from cheating because she writes Alpha males, NOT Alphaholes. (You can figure that one out.) But be careful...she likes her heroes hot and her love scenes hotter. You have been warned...

www.gracegoodwin.com
gracegoodwinauthor@gmail.com

ABOUT GRACE

Grace Goodwin is a *USA Today* and international bestselling author of Sci-Fi & Paranormal romance. Grace believes all women should be treated like princesses, in the bedroom and out of it, and writes love stories where men know how to make their women feel pampered, protected and very well taken care of. Grace hates the snow, loves the mountains (yes, that's a problem) and wishes she could simply download the stories out of her head instead of being forced to type them out. Grace lives in the western US and is a full-time writer, an avid romance reader and an admitted caffeine addict.

ALSO BY GRACE GOODWIN

Interstellar Brides® Books

Mastered by Her Mates

Assigned a Mate

Mated to the Warriors

Claimed by Her Mates

Taken by Her Mates

Mated to the Beast

Tamed by the Beast

Mated to the Vikens

Her Mate's Secret Baby

Mating Fever

Her Viken Mates

Fighting For Their Mate

Her Rogue Mates

Interstellar Brides®: The Colony

Surrender to the Cyborgs

Mated to the Cyborgs

Cyborg Seduction

Her Cyborg Beast

Interstellar Brides®: The Virgins

The Alien's Mate

Claiming His Virgin

His Virgin Mate

His Virgin Bride

Other Books

Their Conquered Bride

Wild Wolf Claiming: A Howl's Romance